NEVER DARE A LADY

With a frown, Wolviston started through the crowd again, determined to find a suitable lady on which to practice his rakish ways.

He glanced toward the entrance as new arrivals stepped into the growing crowd. Three ladies, one in silver, one in gold and one in dark purple, stood for a moment at the door. White masks covered their faces, and cape-like dominos covered their dresses and figures, making it impossible to guess their ages or descriptions.

Wolviston eyed them for a moment and looked away, but something drew his stare back.

The lady in gold glanced around, her eyes shining from behind her mask. She turned, gesturing to her companions, and recognition of those graceful, fluttering movements hit Wolviston like a lead weight on his chest.

Clarissa.

A chill swept across him. If anything happened to her, it would fall on his shoulders. She was here, after all, because he had dared her.

Damn and damn and damn again.

Whatever it took, he had to get her away before she got her chance to meet a real rake.

BOOK YOUR PLACE ON OUR WEBSITE AND MAKE THE READING CONNECTION!

We've created a customized website just for our very special readers, where you can get the inside scoop on everything that's going on with Zebra, Pinnacle and Kensington books.

When you come online, you'll have the exciting opportunity to:

- View covers of upcoming books
- Read sample chapters
- Learn about our future publishing schedule (listed by publication month *and author*)
- Find out when your favorite authors will be visiting a city near you
- Search for and order backlist books from our online catalog
- Check out author bios and background information
- Send e-mail to your favorite authors
- Meet the Kensington staff online
- Join us in weekly chats with authors, readers and other guests
- Get writing guidelines
- AND MUCH MORE!

Visit our website at
http://www.zebrabooks.com

A DANGEROUS COMPROMISE

Shannon Donnelly

ZEBRA BOOKS
Kensington Publishing Corp.
http://www.zebrabooks.com

This one is for Sammy,
my very own rakish rogue

One

At first it seemed only his just reward for eaves-dropping, however unintentionally. But then they began to tear into him in earnest, and an affronted anger began to simmer inside Lord Wolviston's chest.

He had come out into the garden for a moment's escape from the noise of a hundred voices, all trying to be heard over the violins scraping and the glasses clinking and the laughter trilling. He'd had a physical ache in his chest—as if some great monster had sat on him, keeping him from breathing. He had fled Lady Havers's ballroom, using his height and wide shoulders to push through the crowd. The heat of too many dazzling candles and the assault of too many perfumes made him want to drag the high, starched cravat from his neck and unbutton the stiff brocade waistcoat that lay under his fitted black coat.

Had it been this awful nine years ago? He had vague memories of his few days on the town—his short fortnight of precious freedom before responsibility had crashed down on him in the form of his father's crippling accident.

Now, that particular weight was gone—lifted with his father's merciful passing. With the boys off to university, and his mother settled with Cousin Martha, he had come to London to kick up his heels—while he still had enough life to do so. Instead, he was learning that he was a stuffy, dull fellow with no graces or attractions.

He knew that he must be, for two young ladies were saying just that.

Young ladies, Wolviston thought with a sour twist of his mouth. Young cats, more like, out to sharpen their claws on him, and they had not even met him face-to-face.

The damnable part was that he knew who they were. Only he was a gentleman. He could not embarrass them all by stepping out from behind the lone, newly-leafed willow tree in the garden and introducing himself to his oldest friend's sister by saying, "Yes, I'm the clod from the country you've just been despising. How nice to meet you as well, Miss Jane Preston."

Oh, yes, that would be a lovely way to pay back the one person who had stayed his friend over long, troubled years.

If there had been any other path back to the house, Wolviston would have turned on his heel and taken it. Instead, he stood under the willow, the darkness screening him, but the heat from his face made him feel like a bloody beacon.

"I tell you, Jane, you must be firm and tell your brother you have no interest in this boring friend of his. The fact that all Reggie could think of to say about him is that he's a viscount is fatal. He's probably fat, fifty. . . ."

"But he can't be fifty if he went to school with Reggie, for Reggie's only eight-and-twenty."

"Yes, but if this old friend has been buried for nine years in Shropshire. . . ."

"Lincolnshire," Jane corrected.

"Well, Wherever-shire, it is all the countryside, and he's bound to act as if he were fifty. He'll have no talk except of pigs and horses. Honestly, Jane, there is nothing more fatal than a brother's friend," the blonde insisted, her light voice firm on the subject.

Wolviston saw her as a silhouette on the dark terrace, slim and outlined by moonlight, so indistinct that only the pale flash of her hair and gown gave her any real form. She was not as tall as Jane, but she was the one leading her friend into scorning him before they had even met. *A shrew*, he decided. If there was any justice in the world, she'd be appropriately sharp-faced. But God help every man in London if that sweet, melodic voice of hers came with looks to match.

"But, Clarissa, you don't have a brother," Jane protested.

"Oh, pooh," Clarissa said, and Wolviston decided that she probably did not allow mere facts to trouble her opinions. "Remember Susan Faraday and how her brother introduced the most perfectly awful old chum? The one she ended up married to? And now where is she?"

There was a pause, then Jane offered, "Sussex?"

"Just my point! She's not in London enjoying life. We must hold to our plan, Jane. Our futures depend upon it."

Curiosity stirred under Wolviston's abraded pride. Plan? Lord, if these two had a plan, it had to be something to make poor Reggie's life miserable.

Wolviston had experience with two younger brothers, and he knew what mischief could lure them off the narrow path of virtue. He couldn't imagine what sort of schemes a female might concoct.

"But, Clarissa, I'm not sure I want a husband who has known dozens of other women. I do not think I should stand up to comparison."

Wolviston scowled at the darkened figures. Now what folly was this girl, Clarissa, stuffing into poor Jane's head?

"That's just the point, Jane. It takes such a man to appreciate your unique qualities because of those comparisons."

Her voice lowered, taking on a wistful longing. "He'll have had his fill of beauties and will be looking for something deeper. He will have known so many women that he will have this extraordinary knowledge of what it is a lady really needs. He will love you as no other man can, and your love for him will save him from himself . . . and from loneliness."

The ache in her voice cut through Wolviston's injured pride. Loneliness. The hollow knowledge of just how lonely life could be lay just under that magical tone. And so did a stirring of passion so pure that he almost wanted to wrap his arms around it— and around her. For a mad instant, he wanted to be the man who could give her what she sought.

Then her voice took up a practical tone, snapping them all back to reality. "Of course, he will have done all his seducing of others long before you will have met, so you won't need to worry about that after your love reforms his ways."

Wolviston almost choked. Bloody hell! This girl

was a menace not only to Reggie's sister but to the world at large with such ridiculous fancies as this. He wanted his arms around her, right enough, so he could throttle some sense into her.

"But just how do I reform a rake?" Jane asked, her voice rising in distress. "I cannot even meet one."

A musical laugh floated into the night, mixing with the sweet scent of mown grass and the hint of coal dust that lay forever in London's air. "Stoopid, you don't have to worry about that. Love will reform him. As to meeting him, well, that is why you have me."

That cut it. Embarrassment or no, he could not allow this wrong-headed girl to lead Reggie's sister down the path to ruin. This chit had less sense than a day-old kitten if she thought to parade Jane before men whose reputations labeled them as womanizers of the worst sort.

Wolviston parted the willow branches and stepped out from its sparse curtain of spring leaves, prepared to confront these silly girls. No sooner had he moved, however, than they, too, turned away and, arms linked, strolled back into the ballroom.

Mouth set in a taut line, Wolviston followed.

Music and heat and an onslaught of scents assaulted him as he opened the doors to Lady Havers's town house.

Along the walls, masses of spring flowers wilted in their enormous Chinese vases. Those not dancing clustered together between the vases, the ladies flirting over their fans and the gentlemen arguing politics or farming or something else over the music. In the center of the parquet floor, dancers, in two long lines, stepped through the intricate measures of a country dance.

Wolviston scanned the ballroom for Jane and her idiotic friend. He stood well over six feet, so he could easily see above the heads of others, although the ostrich feathers that some dowagers wore in their turbans had him twisting and turning for a better view. He caught an inviting stare from one lady, who eyed him over her fan, her dark eyes bold and assessing.

Lovely. I seem to appeal only to the jades of society.

And then he stopped and stared back at her.

Elegant in clinging silk, she smiled at him, sensual knowledge in her eyes and on her curving lips. Obviously, she did not mind that he had spent the past decade or so buried in Lincolnshire. Her stare grew bolder, and he wondered what she saw to make her smile.

He had the usual two eyes—both gray—and one nose, which had taken him forever to grow into. Sun streaks in his brown hair hid most of the gray coming in. He cut his hair when it got in his eyes, and his only vanity was his hands. His father had been so proud that he, of all the boys, had inherited the Fortesque hands—long, tapering, aristocratic.

The lady in the clinging copper silk dress slid the tip of her tongue suggestively over her lush red lips.

Wolviston began to smile, and to flirt with the most outrageous idea he'd had in a dozen years—or perhaps the most outrageous scheme ever to cross his mind.

"God save me from that smile, Evan. It's the one that always ended with me in the headmaster's office beside you, and wishing I'd not listened to you in the first place."

Wolviston turned to find Reggie at his side.

Ginger-haired and stout, Reggie still managed to achieve a fashionable sophistication. Padding in his dark green coat broadened his shoulders, and well-cut black pantaloons almost concealed his fondness for his dinner table. His cravat lay creased in intricate folds, the ends tucked into a richly embroidered waistcoat. If Wolviston had not spent more nights than he could recall sneaking out and back into their rooms at Cambridge, he'd have put Reggie down as one of those fellows who never did anything for fear of ruining his appearance. He knew Reggie far better than that.

"I've been lookin' for you," Reggie said, affecting the slight lisp that marked him as a man who voted with the liberal Whigs, and who followed that hard-living set. "Finally ran m'sister to ground and said I'd present you. Mother's still saying I ought to have brought you by the family home and all, only, trust me, you don't want to go there. You'll get a lecture from m'father on how the country's going to the dogs—I always do—and then m'mother won't let you go until she's gone through your entire family tree, trying to remember exactly who you are. Thank God for the Albany."

Wolviston gave a small smile. He'd allowed Reggie to persuade him to take up rooms at the Albany Hotel, a once great mansion that had been converted into chambers for let. It had become a haven for young men who either did not have a house in London, or who, like Reggie, wished their parents did not. There had been times, over the past three days since he'd come to London, when Wolviston had felt like the old man among Reggie's town companions. And yet they were all about the same age.

"Who the devil has taken up with your sister?" he asked, blunt about it.

Reggie lifted an elegant hand. His exquisite coat did not allow anything so gauche as a shrug, Wolviston guessed.

"Blonde? Pretty as you can stare, and, more than likely, about as much trouble?"

"That sounds a fair description."

"Fair indeed is the golden Miss Clarissa Derhurst. But turn your eyes away from her, Evan. She swears she won't have anything but a rake. Besides, I've marked you for Jane, don't you know? Must marry her off sometime, as Mother keeps saying. And why not to you, eh, old man?" Reggie grinned.

Wolviston shot him a narrowed glance. "If you don't mind waiting five or ten years, I shall think about it. Meanwhile, I am going to actually live some of my own life while I can. And, if you're not careful, your sister's going to end up wed to some blackguard. Or worse, she'll end with her reputation ruined and her virtue lost if this Clarissa has her way."

Frowning, Reggie stared down at the wineglass in his hand. He swirled the burgundy. "Why the devil do you think I was so all-fired pleased to see you come to town—besides the joy of seeing your face? Thought you might at least turn their heads."

Wolviston gave a derisive snort. "Oh, I've turned them, all right. Turned them quite away. For all my title, seems your Clarissa has already declared that I am a country squire with manure on my boots and about as much address as those flowers beside you."

He knew he sounded as if it bothered him that she had discarded him sight unseen. But what did the opinion of a slip of a girl matter to him? There was no damnable reason why the scorn in that melodic voice should haunt him. But it did, festering like a sliver lodged under his skin.

He turned back to the room and caught sight of Clarissa and Jane.

The golden-haired Clarissa wore yellow, pale yellow that made her hair glint a much deeper gold. The high-waisted gown hinted at a trim waist and well-rounded hips, and was cut low enough to show the tantalizing shadow between sweetly curved breasts.

She was too short, he decided. But she would just fit into a fellow's arms, with her head coming to rest on his shoulder and those curves tucked nicely into reach.

Well, then, perhaps those same curves would become too plump over time. Although he could not help noticing the elegant curve of her neck and how her slender wrists hinted instead at a figure slimmed of girlhood curves and grown into exquisite ripeness.

He frowned. Well, at least, fair hair had never appealed to him. But he had to admit that the range of gold in her curls, from straw at the tips to the rich hue of sun-ripened wheat closer to her face, might well captivate any man.

Scowling, he searched for some other sign of the shrew he had heard.

A heart-shaped face tapered to a rounded chin,

and he thought he detected a hint of stubborn tilt there. Dark lashes framed intensely blue eyes, and light brown eyebrows kissed with the faintest gold arched over those eyes in a lovely sweep of color against her pale skin. And there it was, that flaw. Two, in fact.

While she listened to the gentlemen crowded around her, those blue eyes never brightened with real interest. And those perfect lips were not quite perfect, for the lower one seemed a touch fuller, a touch more sensual, and never quite curved in a real smile.

She kept Jane close beside her, but not, it seemed, for comparison. No, he had heard genuine affection in their voices when they had spoken on the terrace. But Jane certainly did not shine next to her fair-headed companion.

Jane's reddish-brown hair seemed ordinary next to Clarissa's glorious curls. Her slim form seemed too thin, and she looked too tall next to Clarissa's petite perfection. She also looked as if she wished she could will herself to fade into the background.

Even though he resisted, Wolviston found his stare drawn back to Clarissa. He detested her for involving Reggie's sister in her schemes. And he disliked her even more for fascinating him.

"Can't your mother—or better still, her own—put a leash on her?" he growled to Reggie. The ball-room seemed hotter than ever, and he shifted, uncomfortable in his own skin.

"Her mother's an invalid or some such thing. Father's dead—self-defense, no doubt. I think an aunt was supposed to bring her out in the world, but she's breeding—the aunt, that is—so the beauty's under

the wing of her widowed godmother. Lady Havers,"
he added, his tone glum.

"Oh, Lord help us," Wolviston said, meaning
every word as a true prayer.

His mother had been slightly acquainted with
Lady Havers years ago, and he could still hear his
mother's disdain for that lady's lack of wit or sense.
Lady Havers had married a rake, he seemed to recall—a man who now really was raking over the coals
of hell, if that wives' tale was true. But with Lord
Havers long ago dead, perhaps her ladyship had remade his memory into a more romantic one—one
that was too alluring for her foolish goddaughter?

"She's been spoiling both of 'em," Reggie said.
"With shopping trips and every treat she, or they,
can think of. And Clarissa seems able to think of
quite a few."

"Why does your mother allow it?"

"Well, don't look at me like that. I'm not the head
of my family. Mother's so relieved that Jane's even
willing to go out that she don't want to say a word.
And Father does what she tells him to. For a time,
old fellow, we thought Jane might lock herself up
in the stables with her horses and simply refuse to
come out and be presented to the world. Clarissa's
been the only one who could coax her to do the
pretty at all."

Wolviston gave a tight smile. "I see why you
thought Jane would suit me for a wife. We'd be oh
so comfortable together in the countryside with our
horses and pigs."

"Pigs?" Reggie's face flooded an unattractive red.
"I didn't mean . . . well, I just thought that it would
be . . . well, never mind. Come on, we might as well

get this over with and leave. The food's nearly gone
and so's most of the company worth knowing."

With a glance around the still crowded room,
Wolviston decided that Reggie's idea of thin company was not his. He caught a glimpse again of the
lady in the copper silk gown. Her mouth pulled into
a sulking pout. She turned away to offer him a
glimpse of white back, but then she glanced over
her shoulder with a last smoldering invitation.

It seemed too perfect an opportunity. He had
wanted a lark, and, by heavens, he had more than
one or two left in him. While he was at it, he could
keep an eye on Reggie's sister for him. And, though
he swore to himself it was the least of his reasons,
he had not forgotten the scathing comments that
the fair Clarissa had uttered in the garden. He
pushed down the trepidation that feathered along
his spine at what he was about to do. Damn all, but
he was far enough from following his father to the
grave—or to a stodgy life.

And he'd prove it to her.

"Reggie, old chum, you're not going to introduce
me to your sister."

Stiffening, Reggie eyed Wolviston with dismay.
"That smile is back, Evan. Why do I feel as if this
time it's something worse than stealing a donkey to
ride backwards through the quad?"

Wolviston's smile widened. "You're not going to introduce me, you're going to warn her—and Miss
Derhurst—against me. Tell them that you once knew
me, but I've been on the continent for ages. I had to
flee."

"You did? Why?"

"Well, because of a scandal, of course. Isn't that the curse that dogs every rake?"

Reggie frowned. "What scandal?"

"A duel. Over a lady. A married one, I think. And you're going to do all this while I'm flirting with that attractive lady in the copper silk."

"How do you propose to pull off this hoax? No one's heard of this scandal. Hardly anyone even remembers hearing of you in the first place, you disappeared so utterly from the scene."

"Exactly."

Slowly, a smile spread onto Reggie's round face. "You're a devil, Evan Fortesque. A rogue and a blackguard. But I'll lay you odds that Miss Derhurst tumbles your game before the season's up. She may have an odd kick to her gallop, but she's not dim."

Wolviston grinned. "Oh, I'm not a rogue yet, but I will be. And what odds are you offering?"

Clarissa watched the man who had been talking to Reggie Preston. At first she thought he might be Reggie's friend. But no, how absurd. Reggie's countrified friend, title or no, would not look so attractive in dark evening clothes that fit to perfection, outlining a sleek, masculine form. He would not wear so dashing a gold brocade waistcoat, and he certainly would not have a smile that caught every woman's eye. Nor would he have so reckless a grin. No, Reggie's friend was bound to be more like Lord Morrow, thick and stodgy, and unfortunately dull. Lord Morrow stood next to her now, going on and on about how her ears looked like shells.

She kept smiling, and squashed the urge to ask

him if he meant oysters or clams. She also did not
look up to meet Jane's eyes, for if she did and if
Jane smiled, she would start to giggle and poor Lord
Morrow would ask why and then she would have to
tell him about the oysters and the clams. He was the
third man this week to call her ears shell-like. Jane
and she had been in fits of laughter about the second one last night.

Her eyes, of course, they all called ''limpid
pools''—Jane had asked if they ever mentioned al-
gae, which had set Clarissa off again. Then came
the peaches on her cheeks, and the golden wheat
of her hair, and on and on until she wondered if
they would rather harvest her instead of court her.

She had hoped for so much better—at least more
exciting—from her first season in Society when
she'd arrived in London three weeks ago.

She risked a glance at Jane, just to ensure that
her friend was actually talking to someone. She
was—to Sir Anthony Lee—and a smile curled up inside Clarissa. Even if Sir Anthony was a bit old—for
he was all of four-and-thirty—he had polish enough
not to ignore Jane. She'd had to remind more than
one of her admirers to address Jane, and she was
starting to be quite out of humor with those who
acted as if Jane did not exist.

Looking around her, Clarissa again sought out the
gentleman who had been with Reggie. Who was he?
Where was he? Ah, there, talking to Lady Carroll.
And smiling in such a warm way that it had Clarissa's
stomach knotted. She frowned as he touched a finger to Lady Carroll's bare arm and then let his touch
glide down her skin.

Clarissa turned away, unaccountably cross, and to

make up for her ill-humor she smiled brilliantly at Lord Morrow. He left off talking about shells and simply stared at her, his mouth agape. Clarissa glanced back at Lady Carroll, unable to resist the urge to see what he was doing now.

Who was he?

The sun had streaked interesting colors into his brown hair, so that it looked almost like polished walnut. He wore his hair longer than was the fashion, and it curled softly around his ears and the nape of his neck. She could not see the color of his eyes, for he stood profile to her, but she liked that strong, firm chin and that lovely nose.

And, if she were utterly honest with herself—which she tried very hard to be—he had caught her interest by ignoring her.

He had not ignored her completely. No man did. She had accepted that fact at so early an age that she could not even remember a time when people did not stare at her and remark on her looks. She had grown accustomed to that. However, she had noticed him watching her. But then he had gone to Lady Carroll's side. That irritated her, and she was ashamed to acknowledge that an itch of jealousy lay hot in her chest.

You can't always have your own way, dear. And when you learn that, you will have taken your first steps toward really growing up.

Aunt Maeve's words echoed in Clarissa's mind. At the time that Lady Rothe had spoken them, she had been standing on the steps to Rothe House, one hand pressed to her expectant form as she saw Clarissa off. However much she adored her aunt, that advice had annoyed Clarissa enormously. She was, after all, nearly nineteen. The gentlemen around York had been acting as if she were fully grown—and trying to kiss her—since she was barely sixteen.

But then she had spent the carriage ride to London thinking about those words, alternately vowing to show her aunt—and her uncle, and even her mother—how grown up she was, and then being utterly terrified that she was not at all old enough, or wise enough, or anything enough for smart London Society.

She glanced back at Lady Carroll, with her silk dress that revealed her figure, and her desperate eyes and her hard mouth. A chill chased along the back of Clarissa's neck. She did not want to become hard like Lady Carroll. No, she would not.

And neither would Jane.

They would marry for love. For passion. Just as her own godmama had. And she and Jane would be happy.

She turned back to Lord Morrow, determined to make up for her drifting attention by listening to him go on about her ears for a while longer, but another voice interrupted.

"Hallo, Morrow, what's all this about shellfish? Haven't you eaten yet?"

Clarissa's smile became real. "Reggie, Lord Morrow was just being sweet and paying me nice compliments. But you must excuse us, my lord," she said, taking Reggie's arm and almost dragging him to the edge of her court where Jane stood. "In fact, you all must excuse us, please."

With some grumbling, the other gentlemen took their leave.

Reggie extracted his arm from Clarissa's grip.

"Don't know how you manage 'em all. Did you take a course on lion taming or some such thing at that school you went to with Jane?"

"I had to learn how to manage my uncle when he came to be my guardian, and that was training enough," Clarissa said, and then dimpled up at him. "He, you see, actually is a lion."

"Not one of these tame tabbies, you mean?"

"I did not say so," Clarissa said. "But, speaking of such, have you come to drag Jane and myself off to meet your friend from Lincolnshire?"

Reggie's face blanked. Clarissa tried not to wish that his friend from Lincolnshire had gone back to Lincolnshire. No, she would be pleasant. And if he wanted to talk about horses or pigs, she would put on her most interested face and bear it.

"Uh . . . well. . . ."

"Oh, Reggie, something hasn't happened to him?" Jane asked, her brown eyes soft with worry.

"In a manner of speaking, yes, something has. Seems I was a bit mistaken about his suitability, you see." Reggie launched into the story given him by Evan, warming to it as he went, weaving in details from other affairs and scandals without so much as a single hesitation. After all, he told himself, he was aiming for a political life, and that meant learning how to remake the truth to suit the moment's needs. This was no more than good practice for that.

And both Jane and her friend would be bloody furious with him when they learned the truth. He could hardly wait to see their faces then.

This was just too good an escapade to stay out of. The girls listened to him, their eyes growing larger. Quite gratifying to have them hanging on his every word for a change.

"So you see," Reggie finished, thumbs tucked into his waistcoat pockets and his voice kept stern so he would not laugh, "I can't introduce you to 'the Lone Wolf.' Not the sort of man you should know—if you know what I mean."

Clarissa stood watching Wolviston, excitement warming her from the inside out. She had known it. From the first glance at him, she had felt that small tingle of interest. He stood now, bent over Lady Carroll's wrist, as if helping her with her glove buttons. *Loose glove buttons indeed*, Clarissa thought. An aging London rogue had tried to play that trick with her the other night as an excuse to hold her hand and stroke the inside of her wrist.

Gripping her fan, she exchanged a speaking glance with Jane, who stared back, her eyes a touch alarmed.

"Our first rake," Clarissa mouthed silently to Jane.

Jane's face flooded with red, but before she could answer, Reggie took hold of her arm.

"Come along, Jane. Mother's been wanting to go home this past hour. Miss Derhurst, do give Lady Havers our regards."

"I shall see you tomorrow," Jane said, and then she leaned close to brush her lips to Clarissa's cheek as she whispered, "Promise me you won't do anything until after we can talk."

For an instant, mutiny rose in Clarissa's chest. Not do anything? With him in the same room, and when she might not have another chance? But the pleading in Jane's eyes forced Clarissa to smile and squeeze her friend's hands.

"I promise," Clarissa vowed, and crossed her fingers in their secret sign to show that she meant it.

She watched Reggie escort Jane from the room, then turned to see if she could find her godmother, but as she did, a large chest loomed before her. Her gaze rose from the gold brocade waistcoat, framed by a black coat, to the white cravat, and up to that attractive face.

Oh, his eyes are gray. Gray with gold flecks, she thought, that tingle spreading across her skin as it had when she had first glimpsed him.

"Miss Derhurst," he said, and she knew that he should not, for they had not been introduced. He had presumed to address her as if he had been presented to her as someone suitable to acknowledge. She ought to turn away. She ought not to answer him.

And then he asked, his deep voice brushing over her like a warm hand, "May I have this dance?"

Two

For an instant, Clarissa could not say anything. If she did, she was afraid it would be an all-too-eager *Yes, please*.

She wet her lips and reminded herself of the promise made to Jane. Dancing with Wolviston fell, unfortunately, into that category of "doing something." And so she really must not.

Lifting her chin, she stared back at him, hoping that he would not notice how rapid the pulse fluttered in her neck. And very much afraid that she did not look the confident lady she wanted to be, but instead appeared to be what she was—a girl from the wilds of Yorkshire with no sophistication, and no clinging copper silk dress to entice him.

She tried on a smile, and then said, "I can hardly give you this dance when no one has given me your name."

For an instant, his gray eyes hardened and his lips formed a cynical smile. *Oh, I've done something stupid,* she thought, her heart falling down to a pit in her stomach. Society held so many rules. Did he think her provincial for making a fuss out of this minor one, which clearly demanded that he should be introduced to her, or did he think her fast for speaking with him?

She opened her fan to cool her face and instead tangled her gloved fingers with the silk cord that held the ivory sticks to her wrist.

His smile softened. Reaching out, he took her fan from her, then tucked her hand into the crook of his arm. "By all means, let us observe the formalities, but let's not linger here to do so. Another instant and you'll be barricaded behind your admirers, and I don't like crowds."

She glanced around and saw Lord Morrow and half a dozen other gentlemen weaving through the crowd—all, no doubt, intent on asking her for the next dance, or if they could get her a cup of warm punch, or do her some other service. Then she glanced up at Wolviston.

He had not moved. He stood there, his hand covering hers, a curiously intent look in his eyes. Unlike the other men, he was not wearing white evening gloves. His hands—lean and darkened slightly from the sun—spoke of a man who did more than decorate ladies' ballrooms, and his fingers lay over hers, hard and warm and terribly strong.

The breath caught in her chest and she stared up at him, her lips parted, trying to read what emotion lay in those stormy gray eyes.

This is something important. But she had no idea what she ought to do, or why he was looking at her like that.

And then he looked away and the moment passed as if it had been created from smoke and wishes.

He took her with him through the crowd, guiding her between wide matrons and stout lords, and she had no idea what had just happened, other than that somehow she had lost control of the situation.

Panic flared, but she found at once a quick cure for it by leaping instead to a strong irritation with him. She clung to that feeling, thankful to have stepped back out of those unknown sensations of a moment before.

Gentlemen, she knew, did not care to be managed, but they so terribly needed it. At least her own father had. As an only child with a mother who took to her bed over the least crisis, she had learned to manage her father quite well. Of course, all that had fallen apart when her father had died. And her uncle—her guardian—had been another matter. He had been most reluctant to let her come to London. However, in the long run, she knew how to get what she wanted, and she knew her own mind as to what she wanted.

Or she had until an instant ago.

Now this Wolviston was dragging her off with him and she could not stop him. Reggie Preston had warned that Wolviston had an unsavory past, so she had better take care.

He led her into the supper room, which lay adjacent to the main ballroom, connected by gilt double-doors. Footmen and maids in the dark blue livery of Havers House glanced up, startled from their work of clearing away the used plates and demolished remnants of the midnight supper, which had actually been set out closer to three in the morning.

Ignoring them, Wolviston led her to a pair of chairs near the fireplace, which lay in the shadows of guttering beeswax candles. The servants went back to their work, their voices hushed as they spoke to each other. Clarissa sat down. Wolviston really had left her with no other choice, and besides, she was curious now. This seemed an odd place for a seduction.

Wolviston, still standing, gave her a deep court bow. "Allow me to present myself. I am Evan Oliver James Charles Fortesque, Viscount Wolviston, Baron Saltfleet, and you are welcome to make free with any of my names that suit your fancy."

Ducking her chin, she tried to hide her smile. He really was the most outrageous man to have swept her away and to be introducing himself in his fashion. And in an empty supper room, of all places.

"And you are Miss Clarissa Derhurst of Yorkshire." He seated himself beside her, so close that he gave off more warmth than did the dying fire. Far closer than was proper. He wore no scent other than the faint, crisp fragrance of starched linen. What a blessed relief that was after Lord Morrow's pomade of spices and rose.

"There, now we are on the most intimate of terms," Wolviston said, smiling at her.

Clarissa folded her hands on her lap. "I would not say that. And no one has introduced you to me as someone I ought to know. Indeed, from what Reggie—I mean Mr. Preston, said, you aren't someone I should know at all."

His gray eyes took on a wicked light. "Oh, I can say for an absolute certainty that Reggie exaggerated my background. What did he tell you?"

"I should not say. That would be gossiping."

"And you don't gossip? You don't care to tear apart another person's character out of that individual's hearing?"

She bit her lower lip. He sounded so harsh, so condemning. "I try not to. It seems that most of what everyone does in London is gossip, only it seems so unfair to the people who are skewered on such sharp tongues."

"Does it now?" he asked, his voice so dry that Clarissa glanced up at him from lowered lashes.

Why did he bring me here if he doesn't like me? she thought, a touch of hurt pride tight in her chest. But then he smiled at her again and she did not know what to think.

He began to play with the tassel on the end of her fan's silk cord. "Such virtue in such a young lady seems rather out of place. Is it your strict moral fiber that keeps you from dancing with me as well?"

Offended, she stiffened. "Now you make me sound as dull as a Methodist. That is not why I would not dance."

"Ah, then perhaps you find me dull? Boring even?" he said, such a hard light in his eyes that she knew his words carried a double meaning, only she could not imagine why.

"No. I—well, it is just that . . . well, I promised Jane."

"Promised her what? Not to dance with me?"

"I promised her not to do anything with you," she answered, her voice sharp.

"And dancing is certainly something."

She gave a sigh. "Yes, and so is everything else."

"You don't sound very happy about it." His smile widened and warmed.

"I'm not. I—" She broke off, biting her lower lip. She almost had said that she wanted to dance with him. And she really couldn't say something that encouraging.

Wolviston smiled. His little beauty sounded cross, and more like the spoilt child she was than the ravishing beauty she looked. But she did not pout. Real disappointment lay in her voice, and he found pity in his heart for her, even though he wanted to go on being harsh with her.

This is how she must do it to everyone else, looking at them with those huge, innocent blue eyes, getting them to forgive her anything.

His hand stopped toying with the silk tassel. "Don't fret, my dear. I won't ask you to break your promises. Not tonight, at least." He rose and pulled her to her feet by her hands. "I shall behave like a perfect gentleman and bestow you back to your godmother, as chaste and pure as when I found you."

She glanced up at him. "Do you find me dull? Is that why you take me back so quickly?"

He looked down at her, surprised that she would ask this. "What odd fancy is this? I thought you knew you were perfection?"

Irritation darkened her eyes to violet. "If you are going to start with flattery then please do take me back to Lady Havers, for there is nothing more boring than that."

"Oh, I'll never flatter you," he vowed, meaning every word. "And while I think it's in you to be many things, I do not think that *dull* is a word which ought to be used in your context."

A frown wrinkled her cream-white forehead. "Why do I feel you are making sport of me?"

"Perhaps because I am. Men and women, after

all, have been making sport with each other for centuries."

"I am not certain I like your kind of sport."

"Then come and enjoy a different one with me tomorrow. Come riding in the park. At one. Before the fashionable arrive." He took her hand again, his longer fingers engulfing her smaller ones. He loomed over her, and she had to lean back to stare up at him. "Or aren't you brave enough?"

Her chin shot up. "I'm not afraid of you."

Letting go of her hand, he brushed the back of one finger to her cheek, his touch as soft as a breeze. "You should be, my beauty."

Then he bowed and left before she could think of an answer; all she could do was put a gloved hand up to the cheek he had touched.

"My dear child," Lady Havers said, bustling up. Plump, with rings flashing on her gloved hands and diamonds glittering on her blue satin gown, she took hold of Clarissa's hand. "Who was that delectable gentleman?"

"Lord Wolviston," Clarissa said, still half in a daze. She blinked and turned to face her godmother. "I'm sorry. I know I should not have spoken to him, but he introduced himself to me and there was nothing I could do."

"Wolviston? Wolviston?" Lady Havers said, her voice vague. She had fair hair, which peeked out from her turban in coy curls, and light brown eyes. She ought, Clarissa knew, to wear glasses, for she was dreadfully nearsighted. But she would only occasionally peer through her lorgnette, which hung from her neck on a strand of pearls. She raised the long-handled glasses now, and watched Wolviston's broad shoulders as he left the rooms.

And then she muttered, "Oh, dear, it looks as if we have run short on champagne again. I must go see . . . oh, but, who did you say he was again? Wolviston? I have heard that name before."

"The family name is Fortesque, and Mr. Preston says that Wolviston is a rake."

Lady Havers's face brightened with interest. "Really? Oh, my dear, I must hear the whole story."

Clarissa hesitated. "I don't know. It seems wrong of me to carry such tales."

"My dear girl, I am your mother's oldest friend, your godmama, and your sponsor in Society. I must know everything about every gentleman you meet—particularly if he is not a gentleman. Now, come, my dear, and tell me all about this delicious Lord Wolviston of yours. And I am certain I will recall somewhere along the line what I have heard about him."

"And what did you tell her?" Jane asked, eyes wide.

The two young ladies sat in the front parlor of Havers House on Berkley Square. Decorated in pale blues and greens, the room seemed to Clarissa a gloomy, cheerless place, but that, she knew, was due in large part to the rain that pelted down outside the velvet curtains.

She turned away from the windows. Surely Lord Wolviston would not think to ride in the park today. Or would his mouth curve in that cynical smile of his, and would he think her poor-spirited to allow the wet to keep her from accepting his challenge to ride?

Clarissa sat down on the sofa next to Jane. Magazines littered the floor around them.

"What could I do but tell her everything that Reggie told us? I vow, the tips of my ears burned the entire time, and I could not help but remember Wolviston's scorn when I told him that I did not like to gossip." She sat up. "Do you know, I think he's been dreadfully wounded by the gossip about him. I think he is too proud to show that he feels Society's scorn, but that it burns in his heart like a brand."

Jane put her head to one side and considered. "I don't think I should mind being scorned if I wasn't in London to actually be there for the scorning. And he certainly has not been much in London."

Propping her chin on her hand, Clarissa stared into the fire. "Yes, but men are so fussy when it comes to notions of pride and honor and name and all that. We women are far more practical."

Jane frowned. "Are you saying we women are not honorable?"

Rolling her eyes, Clarissa leaned back against the brocade. "No, silly. Of course we have honor. But would you arrange to meet another woman at dawn, on a mist-covered moor to shoot at each other for some spoken insult?"

"Of course not." Jane dimpled. "Noon is a far better hour to meet. And I should request needles as my choice of weapon—you know how deadly I am with sewing."

Clarissa dissolved in giggles at the thought of Jane and herself squared off like fencers, each armed with inch-long needles. She tried to sober, and reminded Jane sternly, "Now you have to be serious about this. It is our futures at stake here."

"No. Not mine. I've made up my mind. I don't want a rake for a husband."

Clarissa sat upright. "Don't want? . . . But how can you say that? You want romance in your life?"

"Well, I. . . ."

"And adventure?"

"I do, but. . . ."

"And a man who will love you to distraction?"

"No, I don't. Not if it means he will be pestering me so much that that's why I'll be distracted."

Standing, Clarissa loomed over her friend. "Jane Preston, look at me and swear you will be happy with a dull country squire, and I will immediately seek out your brother to see what other old, honestly dull friends he has lurking in his past."

Jane sat still, staring down at her hands and twisting her fingers together. Clarissa knelt beside her friend, and covered Jane's hands with her own.

"Remember what we vowed to each other when we were reading my namesake book?"

Jane nodded.

"And remember how we each said that the Clarissa in that book was a silly ninny to starve herself to death when she might have married the rake who ruined her, and could have lived perfectly happily ever after? Did we not say we would have handled that situation far better?"

Jane nodded again, and then glanced up. "But I . . . well, Lord Wolviston is so . . . so awfully tall and, well, large. He is rather intimidating, don't you think?"

"Nonsense," Clarissa said with a toss of one hand.

"He is a man with a scarred heart and a wounded past—that is what Lady Havers swears makes a rake, you know. They all have some dreadful secret. So, of course he will seem intimidating at first." She smiled. "Deliciously so. But he really is no more difficult than any man. Honestly, Jane."

Noticing the mulish turn to Jane's mouth, Clarissa let out a small, silent sigh of relief. She had vowed to herself not to be selfish, but it looked as if Jane's heart was not involved in this matter. Which left the field happily open to her.

"If you prefer, Jane, he will be my rake. And we will look for another one for you."

Jane's face brightened and her smile warmed Clarissa's heart. *This is how some man must see her someday, and the man who can make my sweet Jane smile like this—he's the one I'll see her wed.*

"Would that really be all right with you?" Jane asked, her expression doubtful. "I mean, you don't mind taking Wolviston?"

Getting up, Clarissa strode back to the window. She did not trust her face to remain as indifferent as she tried to make her voice. "Well, as to that, we must see what transpires. After all, we know practically nothing about him just yet, other than some rumors from your brother. Wolviston may not be a rake who can be reformed. In that case, we must both set him aside. And there is always the chance that he will not fall in love with me."

She frowned, thinking of how he had treated her last night. He certainly had not acted as if he were smitten by her. And yet he had sought her out. Why? What did he want from her?

Clarissa heard the rustle of Jane's petticoats and

skirts as she rose and came to the window. Jane wrapped her arms around Clarissa. "Stoopid. Of course he must fall in love with you—everyone does. And then he will open his heart to you, and you will fall in love with him as well. I am certain of it."

Leaning back, Clarissa held on tightly to her dear friend's warmth and certainty. *But will he really fall in love with me? Or will he, like all the others, love only the beauty that must fade one day?* She knew all too much about such surface affection. Ah, well, the proof indeed would be if Wolviston could be brought to open his heart to her.

A week's hard rain reminded London that winter had not yet finished, even though the first official day of spring had already come and gone. And Evan found himself, for the first time in his life, fretting about the weather. He had been happy enough at home in the country for a week of rain that would keep him inside with his brothers, or a good book, for company. So why should this be different?

It was not, he told himself, that he wanted to see the Derhurst girl again. He had only to attend any ball, or some Drury Lane play, to see her, and see her surrounded by her admirers. But that wasn't a sight to interest him. Far better to wait until she could ride with him. If she would.

And if she didn't, he would then hunt her down at some event and tease her mercilessly about it, he decided.

In the meantime, he sought advice about developing rakish habits.

"It's quite easy," Reggie had said. "Just drink too

much, gamble even more, I can take you 'round to the dens of iniquity, and then don't give a damn about your dress and you'll be quite rakish. But, don't, my good fellow, be seen at Almack's. Lot of high-sticklers there, so it's not the sort of place a rake will get a ticket for."

"You're a fine one to advise me," Wolviston said, easing himself into his waistcoat and then turning to button it. "You stand to win fifty pounds if I don't pass muster as a rogue."

Sitting up, Reggie helped himself to the toast off Wolviston's breakfast table. "Well, it's not as if you can advertise for a rakish-tutor, old son. Besides, I'm only making sure you have a sporting chance. Don't want you saying I won due to the unfair advantage that you're such a green one."

Wolviston gave a snort and then allowed his man, Shadwick, to help him into his coat. He had just straightened his cuffs when Shadwick's discreet throat-clearing caught his attention.

"Yes, what is it?"

"May I suggest, m'lord, that if it is a rakish appearance you desire, you might affect a black cravat. Something silky, which would almost invite a lady's touch to untie it."

Wolviston found his face warming at such an image. He eyed his valet. He had hired the fellow from an advertisement in the *Times*, but he hadn't bothered to check the fellow's references, and now he began to wonder if he should have.

"And how is it that you know so much about rakes?" Wolviston asked.

"I had, m'lord, the dubious honor of being in the employ of the Earl of St. Albans."

Reggie sat up, his toast forgotten. "St. Albans? The devil you say! That fellow has the worst sort of reputation."

"Shadwick, I don't recall that name being on your list of references," Wolviston said, folding his arms and studying his valet.

Slim and slight, the man looked more like an accountant than a valet, with a narrow face and receding dark hair. He dressed neatly in black, his clothes molded to him in an impressive fit. It had been the style and quality of his dress that had recommended him most to Wolviston, for he was far more accustomed to wearing buckskins, boots, and the same old hunting coat as his daily wear. He'd needed a valet who could give him town polish.

Shadwick shifted from one foot to the other, then fixed his stare on a corner of the ceiling and said, in the voice of one resigned to his fate, "I did not mention him, m'lord, for I doubt he would give me a recommendation to anyone. He turned me off, m'lord, for my interfering in one of his affairs."

"What did you do, man?"

"I disobeyed his instructions and assisted a young miss to escape from one of his lordship's intimate dinner parties."

"Really? And how long were you with St. Albans in total?"

"A mere five months, but it seemed much longer, m'lord. And, now, if you will excuse me, I shall pack my things and. . . ."

"Pack? Why? Did I just dismiss you?"

Shadwick halted and turned a flustered face toward Wolviston. "No, m'lord. But I did withhold information about my past. And I. . . ."

"And you will be extremely useful to me. And you will also tell me only what I ask about your past. I've no wish to go digging into your affairs, any more than I want you digging into mine. But I do trust that if I have any females over for intimate dinners, you will know that I, at least, have either nothing but honorable intentions, or they have nothing but dishonorable ones."

Shadwick's color faded back to his more normal white. He gave a small bow. "Of course, m'lord. You are a gentleman. However, should you wish for a more rakish appearance, I would still recommend that black cravat."

Turning, Wolviston studied his appearance in the mirror. Something silky. He could almost picture slim, elegant hands caressing the fine silk, tugging at it, loosening it. He smiled. "Yes. I'll wear it to ride in the park, I think."

Clarissa's gray gelding fretted under her, side-stepping across Rotten Row. Billowing clouds hung in the sky, dancing shadows across the soggy grass and then parting to reveal wan spring sunlight. The ground lay muddy between the wooden rails that separated the row's riding lane from the green of Hyde Park, but it wasn't raining. However, Clarissa's mood was as uncertain as the sky.

It irritated her that Jane had refused to come riding. Jane always looked her best on horseback, and Clarissa had wanted her friend to show off a little. But Jane had glanced uncertainly at the sleepy groom provided by Clarissa's godmother—and hand-picked by Clarissa—and had decided that she really should not go riding to meet a known rake.

"Really, Jane, do you expect him to ravish you on horseback? If he could, he would be making a fortune at Astley's. He's a rake, not a performing equestrian!"

But no arguments would persuade Jane, and so Clarissa set out with only the sleepy groom for company, more determined than ever to meet Lord Wolviston.

And I am not nervous about meeting him, she told herself fiercely. Then she scowled at her mount and said, "Duff, you may behave yourself, sir."

The gray settled back into a placid walk. Clarissa scanned the park again. She had arrived just after one, for she had not wanted to appear too eager. Now she wondered if she had missed him. Oh, why had she come at all? Perhaps she should have heeded Jane's caution. After all, he had not come to any of the amusements she had attended over the past few evenings. Obviously, he was not that interested in her. Was he?

Duff danced again under her tight rein, and she forced herself to relax. She was making him fidgety. But it was not because she was apprehensive. No, not at all. She was miffed. Yes, that was it. Jane had been so difficult, and she hated waiting for anyone or anything. She would give him another minute and then she would turn for home.

Five minutes later, she refused to allow disappointment to well inside her. It did not matter to her that he had forgotten their appointment. She would as easily forget him now. She would stop remembering those stormy gray eyes of his, and she would not think about how good he had looked in his evening clothes. And she would stop asking people about his all-too-mysterious past.

Yes, it had all worked out for the best, she decided, her chin resolutely lifted.

But just as she turned Duff for home, she saw a man cantering toward her on what seemed a cloud of blackness and she forgot all her resolutions to forget him.

Three

Wolviston saw the storm warnings halfway across the park. Not in the sky, but in the high tilt of that beautiful, stubborn chin and the way Miss Derhurst gave him her excellent profile to admire. He smiled. So the beauty did not like to be kept waiting. Well, it did her no harm to learn some virtues to go with those devastating looks of hers.

Sunlight caught gleams from the golden curls under her plumed hat. She rode well, straight-backed and with a light hand on the reins. A gray riding habit cut in a severe military style clung to her curves, and her horse's mincing steps moved those curves in interesting ways. It was a damn good thing he was not a rake, for she made a luscious enough picture to tempt any man into finding a secluded, tree-sheltered corner of the park for an encounter more intimate than a morning ride.

He brought his black gelding into step next to her gray and noticed that he had miscalculated in one respect. He should have ridden a shorter horse. Mandrake's lean form towered over the gray. Clarissa had to tilt her head up to look at him, and that, he saw from another flash of irritation in her eyes, did nothing to improve her humor.

He gave her a smile and as good a bow as he could manage from a saddle. "Good morning, fair beauty. Ah, but I forgot. You don't like compliments, do you?"

With a curt nod, she turned back to admiring the park. "Why, Lord Wolviston, what a surprise to see you. I had quite forgotten that you had mentioned something about a ride in the park. Unfortunately, I was about to go home."

"Liar," he muttered as the horses walked alongside.

She pulled her gray to a halt and swung around in her side-saddle to face him. "What did you say?"

He halted his own mount. "You heard me. Your groom over there looks bored into somnolence, so I can only gather that you must have been waiting some time for my arrival."

For an instant, her eyes flashed like indigo sapphires and color flagged her cheeks. *My god, she looks magnificent like this,* he thought, and images cascaded into his mind of other ways to kindle that fire in her eyes.

Then anger dimpled into utter mischief, and his head spun. Lord, no wonder she'd been spoilt. The combination she presented of lethal beauty, bold passion, and innocent charm seemed designed to devastate any man. He found his own resolve to teach her a few much-needed lessons weakening. It was only the echo of her scorn from the garden that gave him the resolve to look away from her, and remember his vow.

She's a spoilt beauty, but by heavens she'll learn that there is at least one man in the world who will not succumb to her tricks, he swore to himself.

"That was not a lie," she said, and then urged her mount forward again to a brisk walk. "I was about to go home."

He brought Mandrake into pace with her and gave a measuring glance down at the perfect profile she had presented to him. "So you had forgotten our ride?"

She looked up at him, a hint of a pout on her lips. "It is rather that you seem to have forgotten me. I haven't seen you once these past few evenings."

"How would you know if I had been near? In the crowd of gentlemen around you, one more is far too easily overlooked."

She dropped her stare. "You are not so easy to overlook."

His glance sharpened. He shifted in his saddle and Mandrake danced a little until he settled the gelding. He had to remember that his little beauty wanted a flirtation with a rake. There was no honest sentiment in what she said. If she knew that he was as tedious as she had branded him, she would have no sweet phrases for him.

"So you have missed me?" he said, forcing his tone to remain light.

She looked at him, her chin up again. "I did not say that. After all, a man with a humpback is hard to overlook as well."

He gave a laugh. "Ah, it's my damaged reputation that makes me stand out in a crowd then?"

"You have no reputation that I seem able to discover. Reggie Preston seems to be the only one who knows anything about you, in fact."

His grin widened. "You have been asking others about me, then? This grows better and better."

Clarissa pressed her lips together before she said anything else that led him to exaggerate her interest in him. He rode well, she noted with a perverse irritation. Rakes were supposed to flirt well, dance beautifully, and be able to make love to perfection. She had not thought about them in any other context, and to see Wolviston in the park, astride that magnificent black horse, did not fit with her notion of a rake.

She realized with a flush of embarrassment that she had not thought about her rake as existing outside the context of a ballroom. It was a little annoying to have to remake her ideal.

As he rode next to her, controlling the large, dark animal with a light hand, admiration wormed its way into her vexation. Drat the man. Why did he not act as she expected him to?

His horse bumped up against Duff, so that Wolviston's knee brushed against her thigh, and he leaned close to ask, "Tell me, what else have you been thinking about me?"

She turned and tilted her head, as if considering. She very much wanted this meeting to be back in her control and going the way it was supposed to. She had pictured him coaxing her, paying her lavish compliments that she would deflect with poise and intriguing mystery. Instead, she felt, well, she felt very much off balance and on the defensive.

It was time to change that.

Eyes narrowed, she announced, "I have been thinking that perhaps you are a fraud."

His hand tightened, halting his black gelding, making the animal toss its head in impatience. He stared at her, his expression blank, and she knew that she had at last gotten the upper hand. She urged Duff forward, came about, and then halted next to the black so that the two horses stood head to tail and she could look Wolviston full in the face.

Wolviston sat there stunned, wondering how he had given himself away. Or had someone said something to her?

Then mischief warmed Clarissa's eyes. "You are a fraud and a phantom, are you not? In fact, you do not seem to exist. You sprang to life by magic. And you shall vanish just as easily."

He smiled at her, then leaned closer. "If I do not exist, does that mean if I kiss you that my kiss does not exist either?"

Side-stepping her horse away from his, she wheeled him around and glanced back at Wolviston. "I thought we came to ride." With a laugh, she set her horse into a light canter.

He spurred Mandrake forward and they rode down the path together. The hoofbeats of her groom's horse echoed distantly behind them, and the cold wind stung color into Clarissa's cheeks. She urged her mount faster. He kept pace with her until she pulled to a halt, her breath rapid, her eyes laughing, and he honestly would have liked to have stolen a kiss from those lush, parted lips.

Instead, he asked, "And how is it to ride with a phantom?"

She gave a small shrug. "Well enough. Now, tell me, Lord Wolviston, where is it that phantoms spring from? Besides on the Continent?"

He frowned, and Clarissa wondered if she had touched a sore memory. She should not have said anything, but curiosity ate at her, pecking away at her manners.

"I buried myself in the countryside for the past decade," he said.

She gave him a pout. "You are teasing me."

"Very well, then. I've roamed the world, finding empty pleasures and hollow amusement. Does that better fit your notions of what you wish me to be?"

Her pout deepened. "You are still teasing me."

Wolviston grinned. He was. And the heady pleasure of having a beautiful woman gaze up at him and give him her full attention sang in his blood like a chorus of angels.

Angling her head, she gave him a coy look from under the brim of her hat. He judged it a practiced look, but it still had its effect on him, drying his mouth and making his pulse skip lightly.

"Please, will you not tell me more of yourself?"

He almost did. He opened his mouth, and then he realized that mystery served him better than anything else. "Perhaps tomorrow I shall. If you ride with me again." He reached out and pulled her horse to a halt next to Mandrake. "Will you?"

Slowly, the smile warmed her eyes. "Very well. But only if you promise me a new tale every day. A gentleman has a responsibility to keep a lady entertained."

"Well, thank heavens, then, that I'm no gentleman."

They rode together the following day. And the next. And the next after that. They met just inside the Stanhope gate and rode early enough to avoid the fashionable hour of five, when the crush of carriages and riders and those on foot made anything but a sedate walk impossible. He teased her with vague hints of a past that he invented for her, and he enjoyed watching her go through her tricks as she tried to get him to reveal more. It became their game.

And then one day as they neared the Stanhope gate and their good-byes at the end of their ride, she turned to him, her eyes pale and her face troubled. "I will not meet you tomorrow."

Disappointment lurched in his chest, as unexpected as it was sharp. He tried to make light of it. "Are you expecting bad weather, or do you have a better treat in store?"

Glancing down, she fiddled with her dark leather reins. "Neither. I. . . . well, I never see you anywhere else. Never at any balls, or at the opera, or anywhere else."

A pettish hurt lay in her voice, and he almost smiled at it. Except that the hurt sounded real. However, he could not very well tell her that he did not go anywhere because he hardly knew anyone, and no one really knew him, either. His mantel stood bare of invitations, and short of going along with Reggie to events—which seemed an odd thing for a rake to do—he had no way of inviting himself places where she would be.

"So I am a nuisance now?" he said.

She glanced up at him, scowling. "I did not say that. It is just. . . . well, I feel as if you are toying with me. It is as if I am dealing with a mask all the time."

Wary now, he kept his smile fixed. "Perhaps you are."

Clarissa studied his face, trying to decipher what

thoughts lay behind that cynical smile. She did not know what to do with him. She only knew that it was time to put some demands on him to see how he would react. She did not want to think about what she would do if he shrugged and abandoned her forever.

He reached out and tucked one finger under her chin. "If it is an unmasking you seek, then meet me at the masquerade supper at the Opera House, the night after next. At ten, near the main doors. Tickets, I know, can easily be had by any rogue, so I shall hire a box and send you a set."

She lifted her chin from his touch. "And why can you not call upon a lady and offer a proper escort?"

"And what would the world say about you having a rake call upon you? Besides, where is the romance in that? Now, will you meet me, or are you too timid for such an adventure?"

A masquerade. A shiver, part excitement and part fear, chased down her spine. She had heard tell of such events, where a mask gave its wearer the license to dare almost anything, where ladies acted like courtesans and courtesans came dressed as ladies, and where Society forgot its good manners.

Of course she would not allow Wolviston to take any liberties with her. Not yet. But she must think up a costume at once. And one for Jane. And then all she must do was to convince Lady Havers to attend.

With a tap of her whip, she urged her mount forward, then threw back a saucy smile. "Perhaps I shall come. But how would I know you among so many other masks?"

He grinned and called out, "Oh, I shall always know how to find you."

"He ruined her reputation utterly, you know. She had been with him—alone—for over an hour, and the only thing to be done was to send her abroad. He refused to offer marriage."

Clarissa paused outside Lady Havers's drawing room where her ladyship was entertaining. She knew she should knock on the half-open door and announce her presence. Or she should simply go away. But the words, uttered by a sharp-voiced visiting lady, had caught her fast. She stood in the hall, the skirt of her habit clutched in one hand, half-holding her breath. Who had ruined this mystery girl? Surely not Wolviston?

"Did her parents do nothing for her?" Lady Havers asked, her voice both shocked and eager for the rest of the story.

"Oh, there was some talk of legal action—a suit for damages," a third lady said, her voice soft and drawling. "But I heard his solicitors paid off the family. . . ."

"And nothing more came of it," interrupted the sharp-voiced lady. "Lady Byron's departure from Piccadilly Terrace—and the rumors about her husband—quite cast the entire scandal into the shade. The family is now just hoping everyone will forget."

The voices dropped lower.

Clarissa stepped forward, her shoulders tight with anxiety. Who were they speaking of? It could not be Wolviston, could it? A floorboard creaked under her. The ladies broke off their gossip, and Clarissa knew she had best announce herself, rather than be caught in the childish action of eavesdropping on her elders.

Putting on a bland smile, she came into the room, her step light. "Good morning, I—oh, you have callers."

She dropped a dutiful curtsy, and when Lady Havers stretched out a hand to her she came forward and kissed her ladyship's powdered and scented cheek.

"My dear child, back from your ride with color in your cheeks. You know Lady Cowper and Mrs. Drummond Burrell."

Clarissa greeted Lady Havers's guests with the meek respect that she had been taught a young lady should show her elders, but inside a small tremor skittered through her. She knew these ladies. They were among the most powerful in Society. Their opinions swayed others, and they could make her a social success or cause her to be ostracized.

She eyed them warily. Lady Cowper, beautiful and dark-haired, seemed ready to be pleased, but Mrs. Drummond Burrell sat stiff-backed and pinch-faced, looking as sharp-edged as her voice had been.

Clarissa sat next to her godmother, her hands folded on her lap and her eyes downcast as she struggled to keep from blurting out the questions churning inside. Of whom had they been speaking? What man could be so heartless as to have abandoned some poor girl?

The gossip flowed around her, diverting into less interesting channels, and Clarissa clenched her teeth until they ached from the strain of not saying anything.

"You come from Yorkshire, Miss Derhurst?"

Clarissa looked up and realized that Mrs. Drummond Burrell had addressed her and now sat staring at her.

Clarissa glanced at Lady Havers, who gave her a nod that she should answer, and then she said, her voice low, "Yes, ma'am."

"Her mother—my dearest friend—married the previous Lord Rothe, you know." Lady Havers gave a deep sigh and laid a hand across her expansive, lace-covered chest. "Such a tragedy when he died. I vow, my poor Dorothy's health has not been the same since losing her dear husband. But the silver lining in such sorrow is that it gave me the pleasure of launching Clarissa."

"And what a delightful task to bring out such a pretty child," Lady Cowper said, smiling across at Clarissa.

Mrs. Drummond Burrell arched an arrogant eyebrow. "Yes, such an affecting story. But are you quite certain, Lady Havers, that it is really poor health that keeps your Dorothy from London?"

Clarissa stiffened, but Lady Havers waved her hand, as if deflecting the question. "Of course. I mean, she also must be with Lord Rothe's new wife, who is increasing again, you know. And what else could have kept Dorothy from overseeing her daughter's launch?"

With a chilly smile, Mrs. Drummond Burrell confided, "Well, I had heard that the current Lord Rothe married some low creature. A governess, I believe. Thankfully, she has not tried to put herself forward into the world. But I quite feel for your poor Dorothy. I would certainly wish to take to my bed if my family were brought low with such a dreadful mésalliance."

Clarissa listened to this with clenched hands. Then she gave the matron across from her a cold look and said, "Actually, you have it quite wrong, ma'am. Lady Rothe is, unlike others I have met recently, a lady, through and through. And she was my companion, not a mere governess. But she did instruct me that it is the height of bad manners to judge others by anything but how well they act in this world."

Lady Havers uttered a small gasp, and then the room fell into strained silence.

Clarissa's hands trembled, and she knew that she had offended a woman who would probably brand her pert and unsuitable to know. But she did not care. Or mostly she did not. She could not bear to hear such awful things said about her family.

Mrs. Drummond Burrell rose and the other ladies followed, Lady Havers with nervous jumpiness and Lady Cowper with languid interest. Clarissa also stood, for she would not sit and cower. Then Mrs. Drummond Burrell looked directly away from Clarissa, gave Lady Havers the briefest nod, and swept out of the room without looking again at Clarissa.

It was the cut direct. To have been stared at and then looked through as if she had been made of glass. Should they meet again, no doubt Mrs. Drummond Burrell would look away, as if she did not exist. The room spun faintly.

Oh, my word, I've ruined myself without really doing anything.

Lady Cowper came forward with a soft rustle of

her skirts. "It has been a most amusing visit." She glanced at Clarissa. "You really must learn the art of pinking your opponent, my dear. I should hate to lose the pleasure of seeing you take London by storm. Take her in hand, Belinda. Others may not find her so refreshing."

With a smile, she departed.

Lady Havers collapsed back upon the sofa, fanning her face with her open hand, her cheeks red and her breath short. "Oh, my dear. I thought we were done for. Whatever possessed you to speak so to Mrs. Drummond Burrell? Of all the women for you to speak to in that tone! Thank heavens Emily found it amusing to see you set down that horrid, stuffy woman."

"She is horrid," Clarissa said, stiffening. "And I could not sit by and allow her to say that Aunt Maeve is a low creature, and that Mama is not with me because she is ashamed. It is all so unfair and so untrue! And what did Lady Cowper mean about pinking?"

"She meant, my dear child, you must—utterly must—learn to manage yourself. There was—to use Emily's analogy—no need to run that woman through with your barb. A sharp prick is vastly more admired than a bold sweep of a cutting tongue. Oh, my dear, I am having palpitations just remembering it."

Folding her arms, Clarissa slumped onto the sofa. "Well, it does not matter now how I act. Mrs. Horrible-Drummond Burrell will tell everyone—particularly the other patronesses of Almack's—that I am unsuitable, and I shall not get vouchers." She sat up. "And I do not care! And I will show the world that I do not care."

"Don't be silly. Of course you care about Almack's. It is always better to be inside a place than to be left out. But if Lady Cowper is kind she may sway Lady Jersey into allowing us vouchers. Only it is critical, my dear, that you behave very, very well for the next few weeks."

"Weeks? But . . . well, there is a masked dinner and. . . ."

"No. On no condition may you attend any event so dubious as a masque of any sort. We shall go to concerts and affairs of great ton, and we may scrap through this."

"But what of Lord . . . I mean, what of my plan to find a rake and reform him?"

"That must wait, my dear." Lady Havers patted Clarissa's hand and rose. "For the first step is to establish yourself as a young lady of such good credit that your sterling reputation can mend any man's past. It is no good being seen with a rake before the world knows who you are, or you will be ruined instead of him being saved. Now be a good child and run along. I must lay out a strategy for us to recover from this.

"And I really must write to your mother to see if I cannot persuade her to come to town—do you think she might be talked into making the journey? No, no, never mind that. Dorothy hates traveling, I know. Well, we must improvise. And you must be seen to be above reproach."

"Yes, ma'am," Clarissa said dutifully. She walked from the room and shut the door behind her. Then she leaned on the oak door, her head tilted back to stare up at the carved plaster ceiling. A strong sense of injustice welled inside her.

It was not her fault that Mrs. Horrible-Drummond Burrell had been so ghastly. And why must she pay the price for that?

Her eyes narrowed as she studied the intricate plasterwork. Lady Havers had only said that she must be *seen* to be above reproach. So did it not follow that it only mattered that she was not seen at the masquerade?

"Shadwick, what does a rake wear to a masquerade?"

The valet paused in his brushing of Lord Wolviston's evening coat. He straightened and turned to his lordship, who stood in a red brocade dressing gown, staring out the window of his rooms at the Albany.

"There are a number of options, m'lord. Exotic, as in the libertine *Don Giovanni*. Literary, as in Oberon, lord of the fairies. Historic, as in . . ."

"As in I should look a damn fool." Wolviston turned and slumped into a wing chair set before a cheery fire.

"Perhaps not, m'lord. You have the height and shoulder to carry off fancy dress."

Wolviston offered up a lopsided smile. "It is within my limited abilities to act the role of a rake. Add to that yet one more mask and I shall slip and fall. Miss Derhurst has more wit than I first gave her credit for and already she suspects I'm not what I seem." His smile faded and he stared into the fire, remembering their last ride in the park. She had sensed that he did wear a mask, and if he was not careful, Reggie would win his bet. He did not want that. No, he did not want to end his game. Not when he was just starting to really enjoy it.

A muffled throat-clearing pulled Wolviston's attention back to his valet.

"If I may be so bold, m'lord, is there anything I might do to assist?"

Wolviston let out a sigh. Stretching out his slippered feet to the fire, he crossed his ankles and sank deeper into the worn leather chair. "Not unless you can give substance to my shadow. Miss Derhurst called me a phantom, and it seems I am one to Society at least. Reggie's gossip has not spread—a fact that I ought to be grateful for, I suppose."

Only he was not. It rather irked him that he could not even invent a past for himself. Lord, would he go to the grave with a blank headstone?

Frowning, Shadwick asked, "M'lord, I do not mean to pry, but is there nothing of any roguish behavior in your past?"

"Not a thing. Not a blessed thing beyond boyish pranks. I was nineteen when my father's carriage struck a rock in the road. Threw him out and my life with it. It seems I am a dull fellow from the dull countryside."

Only it was not dull. It was damn painful.

He frowned at the fire, memories crowding him of how the village men had brought his father home. A strong, fit man with his legs so mangled that, for an instant, Evan had thought them to be carrying a litter of torn rags.

They had all prayed that night—him, David, Peter, and their mother—that his life might be spared. Then, after his legs had been cut off and his screams had echoed through the house, Wolviston had prayed alone in his room at night that his father might be released from the pain of it. And that had only been the beginning of the ordeal that had dragged into months. And then years.

He let out a sigh and let go the nightmarish images.

That was indeed the sum of his dark secrets—that he had wished his father dead.

And myself as well at times.

He ran a hand over his face. It wasn't like him to be so morose. He had shouldered his duty, to his broken father, and to his even more broken mother, as well as to his younger brothers. He had stayed home to run the estate. He had coaxed and bullied his father into at least enough of a recovery that he had taken an interest in life again, although he had never been able to bear showing his crippled body in public.

After his father's death, he had seen the boys sent to Cambridge, then had settled his mother in the dower house with a sensible cousin who could tolerate her nervous ways.

But why should he feel as if he had been cheated by life? Other men had had worse burdens. So what if he had no hint of scandal in his life? It did not make him a lesser man.

Except perhaps in one woman's eyes.

Getting up, he strode back to the window to stare out at the gathering night and the dark street below.

"M'lord?"

Wolviston turned at the timid inquiry. He gave his valet a smile. Devil take it, he had gone straight from youth to senility if he was worried over what a golden-haired chit thought of his lack of sin.

"M'lord, if I may, I do not mean to deprecate Mr. Preston's service for you in spreading word of your . . . your nefarious deeds. However, I would venture to say that servants's gossip carries a good deal further than any other. If you were to permit me to expand on a few details. For example, your father's tragic accident and how you argued beforehand over . . ."

"But we didn't—"

". . . over your scandalous seduction of a lady. Which, of course, led to your blaming yourself for his accident and to your escape into an empty life of pleasure-seeking."

Wolviston locked stares with his valet, who stared back, his dark eyes placid. Possibilities began to spread before him. With Shadwick's help, he might come out of this farce as a rogue of no ordinary persuasion. His lips quirked. Could he do it? Could he fool the world?

"I am not certain I approve of this dexterity you have with the truth, Shadwick, but I begin to think it might serve quite well."

"Indeed, m'lord."

Wolviston grinned and began to strip off his dressing gown. As he eased into his dark blue evening coat, he said, "There are two more things you may do for me, Shadwick, since you're in such an obliging mood. First, Reggie's already suggested I make a few appearances at some appropriate dens of iniquity. I take it you know of such places?"

He noted Shadwick's disapproving frown and grinned. "Don't look so long-faced. You will not be setting me on the road to ruin. I shall play some cards, drink a bit, and demonstrate a jaded boredom for the more heinous vices available. That alone should make others think the worst of me."

Relief smoothed Shadwick's expression back to its normal blandness. "Thank you, m'lord. And what else might I do?"

Wolviston paused before the mirror to adjust his cuffs, and then put a hand up to smooth the silk of his black cravat. But the picture in his mind was of another hand, slim and delicate, tugging at the silk, loosening it. He frowned. He had more of a rake in him than he had guessed, the way his thoughts turned when they turned toward Clarissa Derhurst.

He pushed aside those reflections, and began to work out with Shadwick just how a rake might set the stage for a dinner at a masquerade.

Four

"Clarissa, will you please stop saying that you have ruined yourself!" Lady Havers put down her knife and fork and stared across the dining table at her goddaughter.

They ate *en famille* this evening, with only the two of them in the white-and-gold dining room. But Lady Havers liked having her good things about her, so they ate from green-patterned Worcester Royal porcelain with green-stained, ivory handled knives and forks.

Picking at the first course of fish, Clarissa gave a deep sigh. "But it is practically true. I have shown myself unworthy of your attention and your trust." She glanced up from under her eyelashes. It was a daring ploy, but the only one she had been able to come up with that afternoon which might get her to the masquerade supper that Wolviston would attend.

Looking irritated, as Clarissa had hoped, Lady Havers demanded, "And what would your mother think if I sent you home when the season has barely begun?"

With a practiced despondency, Clarissa said, "Oh, she would probably think that it was too much to ask you to help me learn the intricacies of London Society. And perhaps it is."

Color bloomed under the rouge on Lady Havers's cheeks. "My dear girl, I have lived in London my entire life. Why should it be too much for me to take you about?"

"Oh, to be sure, she said I would learn a great deal from you. And that you would give me great polish." Clarissa pushed away her uneaten food. "But if you cannot see fit to take me to even a simple masquerade, I might as well wait until my mother and aunt have the time to bring me to London to learn how to deal with such things." She gave another deep sigh, and then clasped her hands tight in her lap and waited.

"Really! Well, I will have you know that your mother and I got into more than our fair share of contretemps when we were girls. And it was I who usually got us out of the scrapes that your mother's impetuous nature led us into. And you are not going to talk me into attending any sort of vulgar masque with this trick, my girl."

Curiosity overcame strategy, and Clarissa glanced up, her interest stirred. "Did my mother really lead you into trouble?"

Flustered, Lady Havers gestured for the courses to be removed. The next dishes were brought out and she helped herself generously from the meats and sauces. "I should not say this—and you must not write to her that I did say so—but I was astonished that your mother seemed content to settle in Yorkshire with your father—but love is mysterious that way."

Clarissa, her stomach growling, selected a slice of

pigeon pie and nibbled on its edges. Attitudes came easy to her, but the show of a lack of appetite at Lady Havers's sumptuous table took almost more fortitude than she could manage. "I supposed I shall end just like my mother—buried in the countryside, and wishing I had had just one real adventure in my life."

She waited a moment, her head lowered in dejection, then glanced up in time to see Lady Havers rise and wave away the footmen who served them.

"Oh, go away and stop gawking," Lady Havers said. Coming around the table, her ladyship sat on the chair next to Clarissa's. When the room cleared, she took Clarissa's hands in hers. "Now, what is all this about? Why should you not want to end like your mother? Was she not happily married?"

Clarissa let out a sigh—this one from her soul. "Oh, I know that Papa loved her in his own way, but . . . well, it seemed as if he never knew how to show her how he felt. She always complained of it, and any little thing has always made her take to her bed, and I know that . . ."

She broke off, her face hot and her stomach knotted.

"Know what, my dear? Come now, you may speak as if I were family, for I have known your mother far longer than you have."

"It is just . . . I've overheard the doctors say that there never is anything really wrong with her."

"No, there never has been. Dorothy always did take to her bed whenever she wished to avoid things. But I also know that she did indeed fall in love with your father, and she misses him terribly, does she not?"

Clarissa stared down at Lady Havers's aged hands which lay over hers. "I suppose so," she said, but memories pressed on her that made her words hesitant and uncertain. Strained words, tears from her mother, her father's disappointed face. The memories danced across her mind like shadows from a play.

Once, she had run home after being horribly teased by the neighbor's children, who had called her silly and stupid because she would not play with them for fear of ruining her new dress. Seeking out her parents for comfort, she had run straight into a cold argument over her mother's spending on clothes. After watching her mother flee upstairs, her father had turned to her and warned, "You must take care, Clarissa, or you will indeed become as vain as your mother."

His words had struck like a hot poker, coming so hard after the accusations from others that she cared only for her clothing and appearance. She had vowed that she would not become like her mother—a flighty woman who was too much taken up with herself. Only the fear lay close that she could easily become too self-involved, seeking shallow distractions, and indulging in emotional extremes as a replacement for anything deep or real. She could become that if she could not find a deep and genuine passion to save her.

She clutched at Lady Havers's hands. "Oh, please may we go? I can hardly learn anything by sitting at home, now can I? And we shall be masked, so no one will know us. Oh, please, do say we may go just this once?"

A fond smile softened Lady Havers's mouth.

"What is it, really? Are you afraid he will find a prettier face if yours is not there?"

Clarissa frowned. The image sprang up of the woman in copper who had clung to Wolviston's arm. She squirmed in her chair.

Shaking her head, Lady Havers gave a rueful smile. "Ah, I remember that feeling too well. There were times I could have broken this dinner set over my dear Archie's head for his roving eyes, but . . ." She let out a long sigh. "Oh, the way he would make it up to me."

Eager, Clarissa sat up. "Does that mean we may go?"

"Well, for now let us finish dinner. And then we shall talk some more."

And Clarissa, her appetite now truly gone, let out a frustrated breath.

Wolviston sat in a private box on the ground floor of the Opera House. Champagne iced in a silver bucket. An elegant cold supper of dressed crab, buttered lobster, Cornish hens, roast gammon, stuffed artichokes, asparagus in cream, tansy pudding, and saffron cakes decorated the sideboard, along with gold-trimmed plates and gold forks. He had arrived early, at nine, and he was determined to enjoy himself, Clarissa or no Clarissa.

A few discreet guineas slipped to Lady Havers's doorman had produced the news that her ladyship had at first forbidden attendance at the masquerade dinner. She had seemed to change her mind, but the staff at number ten Berkley Square had set to laying odds about whether or not her ladyship would attend.

Wolviston decided he would not wait on any woman's whim. He had already paid for tickets—and sent several to Clarissa—and he saw no reason not to use his own. He needed practice raking, did he not? So he arrived at the Opera House in Covent Garden, with its glitter of a hundred candles and its carnival air. He wore a half-mask over the top of his face and a black domino in the fashion of the Venice masquerades of half a century ago.

Ladies strolled past him, their eyes bold behind their masks and their hips swaying suggestively. Their costumes ranged from the scandalous—with one exposing her figure in the tight-fitting velvet breeches and coat of a boy—to the ridiculous, with another awkwardly struggling to manage the hoop skirts from her grandmother's era.

The men also strolled the crowded floor, rather like predatory animals. Overstuffed predatory animals, Wolviston thought, with disdain for the excess that had left these London rogues ruddy-faced under their masks and wide-bellied under their costumes.

On the opera stage, a small orchestra played a lively Scottish reel. Those who cared to could dance on the cleared floor below the stage. The rest of the floor had been set with round tables and chairs for diners. Laughter and chatter filled the Opera House with noise, and the smell of roasted meats mixed with spices and wine in a heady blend.

Along the walls, in the private boxes, curtains offered those who could afford it the chance for more private encounters. The entire place reeked of sensual decadence. And Wolviston found himself glad that Clarissa had not come.

A fine rake he made, he thought with a twist of his mouth, thinking of a girl's salvation instead of planning her downfall. And it made him feel rather more like the tedious fellow that Clarissa had condemned him as being to realize that the mood around him made him fidget in his chair. Lord, what he wouldn't give to be home by a warm fire with a book.

But, damn it all, he was here to live a little—even if he had to grit his teeth to do so.

Despite his disdain for it—and the faint hint of danger in the dark corners of the house—the mood around him slowly seeped into his skin. He began to wonder what it would be like to have Clarissa here with him, spinning in his arms to some lively tune, her smiling face turned up to his in delight.

But, no. The place was on the edge of respectability and no place for a young lady such as her. He ought to have come first on his own before he'd even dared Clarissa to meet him here. Thank heavens her godmother had enough sense to think twice about such a scheme.

Restless, he put down his champagne and decided to join the milling crowd. He had come here to enjoy it, and that's just what he would do. He would stop holding himself back and join in; perhaps that would stop this damnable feeling that he did not belong in such a place any more than did Clarissa.

On his third tour around the room, his glance caught on a dark-haired shepherdess who sat watching him from her table. She wore no mask, but she had enough paint on her face not to need one. She smiled at him, gave a broad wink, and angled her shoulders to better display her charms. She was attractive in a coarse way, but the thought of having to deal with so much paint left him unmoved.

With a frown, he started through the crowd again, determined to find some suitable lady on which to practice his rakish ways.

He glanced toward the entrance as new arrivals stepped into the growing crowd. Three ladies, one in silver, one in gold, and one in dark purple, stood for a moment at the entrance. White masks covered their faces, and the cape-like dominos over their dresses and figures made it impossible to guess their ages or descriptions.

Wolviston eyed them for a moment and looked away, but something drew his stare back.

The lady in gold glanced around, her eyes shining from behind her mask. As she turned, gesturing to her companions, the recognition of those graceful, fluttering movements hit Wolviston like a lead weight on his chest.

Clarissa.

A chill swept across him. If anything happened to her, it would fall on his shoulders. She was here, after all, because he had dared her.

Damn and damn and damn again.

Whatever it took, he had to get her away before she got her chance to meet a real rake.

Everything had been wonderful, Clarissa thought, scowling at her companion, until the crowd had separated her from Jane and Lady Havers. Then this awful man who smelled of onions had put his arm around her waist and had carried her to the dance floor, and now he would not let her go.

She tried to find Lady Havers or Jane, but the room spun around as her partner twirled her.

"Let go. I don't want to dance," she said, pushing at the man's fleshy hand that held her fast, crushing her domino to her side.

The man, dressed like a cavalier of two hundred years ago, grinned and leaned closer. "Come, sweeting. 'Tis a night for pleasure." He reached up to pull back her domino's hood.

That gave her the chance she needed. She spun away, clutching her mask to her face.

The cavalier pulled her hood away from her hair, but she twisted and the satin domino slipped from his grasp. Heedless of where she was going, she pushed into the crowd. Women laughed as she brushed past them, and men gave her bold stares. Oh, why had she insisted that they must come? And why was Wolviston not here as he had said he would be, she thought, her chest tight with disappointment.

A second pair of arms, strong and firm, caught her up and pulled her away from the press of bodies and into a quiet alcove. Stiffening her arms against him, she turned to face this new assailant, her heart hammering and her nerves strung tight as corset stays.

And then she thought—*Wolviston*. Her heart leapt, but she struggled to put on a show of indifference.

Then her displeasure sharpened. It was not him.

He was tall, like Wolviston. A black silk domino covered his dark evening dress, and he wore a black cravat, negligently tied around his throat. That's why she had mistaken his identity.

However, when he moved, the light from the chandeliers in the center of the Opera House caught on the gold of his hair. As he moved from shadow to light, she stared up at an arrogant, high-bridged nose and an angular, unmasked face.

She drew back, but his hand caught her wrist and then he said, in a faint drawl that sent shivers along her skin, "Ah, my dear, not so fast. I have a desire to see if you have a face to match that glorious golden hair."

Fear hardened in her chest like ice in a river.

Unlike the dancing cavalier, this man was not drunk. At least not that she could tell. And the edge under that smooth drawl told her that this man wanted more than to steal a glimpse of her face.

Wolviston pushed his way toward the door, weaving between the tables, handing tipsy ladies out of his path and putting out steadying hands for gentlemen who were now the worse for too much drink.

By the time he reached the entrance, the ladies were gone. He had no right to feel so angry with Lady Havers for bringing Clarissa here, or with Clarissa for coming, but at the moment, he could have quite cheerfully shaken both of them until any more thoughts of masked events fell out of their minds forever.

As for the third lady, he could only suppose that Clarissa had dragged Jane Preston into this as well. Lord, but that Derhurst chit ought to be locked in a convent for the good of mankind.

He began to pace the floor, looking for his trio of innocents, his temper fraying with every step. And then he heard a lady's piercing voice rise over the noise.

"What do you mean, she is not with you? She was with you an instant ago!"

Wolviston swung around. He pushed past Henry VIII and finally spotted the purple domino. Next to her, the lady in silver stood on tiptoe to see over the crowd. He swept them up, one in each arm, carrying them toward the entrance. Lady Havers's wider girth identified her as the one in purple.

"I beg your pardon," she said, bristling. "But what . . ."

"Lady Havers, Miss Preston, I beg pardon, but you will come with me," he said, sweeping them forward, even though their slippers seemed to stick against the floor.

Lady Havers huffed and Jane Preston shrank back and trembled, but he bore both ladies with him. When he had them both in an alcove near the entrance, he let them go. Pulling off his mask, he demanded, "Where is Clarissa?"

"Wolviston!" Lady Havers said, smoothing her purple domino. "I should have known it would be you. And Clarissa is *Miss Derhurst* to you. I cannot believe she gave you free use of her Christian name."

"And I cannot believe you have let her out of your sight."

"She did not," Jane said. A white mask covered the upper part of her face, but the silver domino had parted, revealing the blush that stained her skin just above her low-cut gown. "That is, we were all turning about, looking around. And then . . . oh, we cannot stand here and argue now. Can you help us find her?"

"Jane!" Lady Havers hissed, turning her face away from Wolviston. "One does not ask a wolf—lone or otherwise—to assist in finding my lost lamb."

Wolviston's mouth twitched. The world should be so lucky as to have a docile, sheep-like Clarissa. "My lady, I would there was a bell about her neck tonight, but you may trust I shall find her even without one."

"Find her to what purpose, I ask, sir?" Lady Havers said, drawing herself up.

"Oh, look—is that her?" Jane said, standing on tiptoe again and gesturing with her fan to a spot not twenty feet away.

Wolviston swung around, his eyes narrowed. Clarissa's golden hair flashed, but Lady Havers's near-fainting gasp and her claw-like grip on his arm pulled his attention back to her.

"What is it now?" he demanded, impatient.

Under the purple satin, Lady Havers's massive chest rose and fell with agitated breaths. Panic made her voice almost squeak. "Not *what*. *Who*. That man with Clarissa—"

Wolviston turned and scanned the area around Clarissa. This time he noticed the golden-haired man who stood in the alcove with Clarissa, his face unmasked.

"It's St. Albans. And I had thought him still out of the country after his last scandal," Lady Havers said, her voice faint and fading.

Frowning, Wolviston remembered his valet's mention of the Earl of St. Albans. The notorious rake, St. Albans.

Cursing softly under his breath, he handed Lady Havers's near-prostrate form to Miss Preston. "Take her ladyship to her carriage. I'll see to Clar . . . to Miss Derhurst."

Jane's masked face turned up to his, her expression fixed by the mask's rigid form, but with her dark eyes showing clear distrust. "I am not certain I hold by the idea that one sets a thief to catch a thief, Lord Wolviston."

"Then be certain, Miss Preston, that my designs on Miss Derhurst do not include allowing another gentleman to play free and easy with her. Now wait for me as I've asked," he said. Then, with a burning in his stomach and his fists clenched, he set off across the floor toward where St. Albans held Clarissa.

Five

The stranger reached for the ties that held her mask in place, but Clarissa stopped his hand with hers. He left her deeply uneasy, and she certainly did not trust him with her identity. Striving for a light tone that would hide any nervous tremor, she said, "The unmasking is not until midnight, sir."

"Oh, I never play by anyone else's rules," he answered, his voice silky.

His gaze roved over her, haughty and assessing. She could not tell the color of his eyes, but only knew that they were pale—and without any hint of warmth. And the insult of being so insolently stared at fired her indignation.

"Sir, if you want to stare at the female form, I recommend you tour Lord Elgin's Grecian marbles."

Her sharp words brought his gaze back to her masked face, and a flash of irritation kindled in those pale eyes. Alarm feathered through her as his mouth tightened into a cruel line.

An instant later, that mouth curved again with a mocking smile. "Marble does not blush so sweetly, nor has it ever offered me such bold quips. But does your face do justice to your other charms?"

Leaning away, she pressed her hand to her mask. "You are hardly a gentleman to so disregard my wish to remain incognita."

"I'm no gentleman at all, but I advise you to surrender to the inevitable, my sweet mystery. I always get my way."

She glared at him. "So do I. And I say you shall not unmask me. And if you do—"

"What? Shall you scream?" he asked, amused.

He pulled her with him into the crowd. Over the scraping violins, a woman's shriek cut the air and then was followed by that same woman's giddy laughter.

"Do scream," he said, his soft, drawling voice in her ear, tickling a shiver into chasing down her spine. "It's been days since I heard a woman do so in my arms."

Staring at the abandoned crowd, her anger drained away and a numbing panic seeped into her legs and arms. She stood in the middle of a room full of people, and yet she was in more danger than if she were in a shadowed and empty London alley.

She tried to bolt, throwing herself forward into the crowd, hoping she would catch him off guard, but that hateful grip locked on her wrist.

"Please—" she said, choking on the word.

"Darling, I don't bite. At least, not very hard."

His smile widened as he pulled her around to face him. She wanted to be ill. She wanted to be back home in bed. She wanted him to be gone.

But then she drew a deep breath.

Crying and sobbing would not help. And she was a Derhurst, after all. Her uncle had served under

Wellington. She would not disgrace her name. She would fight—by fair means or foul.

Facing him, she forced her words out through a fear-tightened throat. "Well, I do bite, sir. And if you do not let go of me, I shall bite and kick and make you very much wish you had let me go."

For an instant, cold appraisal flickered in his eyes. Clarissa held her breath. She waited, tensed and ready to throw an utter fit to gain her freedom.

Then he smiled, his eyes warming for the first time to something almost pleasant. He let her go. "Do you know, I think you would do all those things. But I would really much rather have dinner with you instead."

"And if I say no?"

He shrugged. "Then you are free to leave my company."

She took a hesitant step back from him. He did not reach for her, but the crowd's raucous laughter seemed to close around her. She glanced over her shoulder at the mob assembled. The dancing cavalier raised his glass to her, spilling red wine down his shirt. Next to him, other gentlemen reached for masked ladies, carrying them off to the dance floor, or into curtained rooms.

Glancing back at her former captor, she saw that his cynical smile had vanished. He swept her a courtly bow, always keeping his eyes on her, but now with his hands spread out and his palms toward her. "I can offer you far more genteel company than you will find in other arms tonight, my charming mystery."

She nibbled on her lower lip, then said, "Thank

you, but I am here with friends. Would you be kind enough to help me find them?"

He paused, and then an amused glitter danced in his eyes. "I should be happy to, but only if you first have some champagne with me."

Distrusting that gleam in his eyes, she shook her head. "No. If I go with you, you will pour champagne into me until my head spins, and then you shan't take me anywhere."

His smile widened. "Oh, you are wrong about that. I am at least charmed enough to consider taking you home with me to find out what else you are behind that mask, other than intriguing."

He reached for her again, and this time, she feared, if he took hold of her, she might not get away. Before she could act, a shepherdess—dark-haired and laughing—careened into his arms, making him stagger, so that he had to catch her to keep himself and the shepherdess from falling.

Without waiting to see more, Clarissa turned and fled into the crowd, only to find herself swept away once again by a man's strong arms.

Anger and fear fired in her blood. She'd had enough of being pawed. She dug her elbow into this new assailant's ribs and demanded, "Let go!"

He let out a soft grunt, and then leaned over her and said, his voice strained but recognizable, "That's poor thanks for sending that shepherdess to save you from St. Albans's clutches."

"Wolviston!" She clutched at his arm. Embarrassing tears stung the back of her eyes and an absurd illusion of safety swept over her. Which was utter nonsense, for he was a rake, was he not? Yet she wanted nothing so much as to bury herself against his broad chest and snuggle close to his warmth.

She struggled to summon a sense of outrage that he was handling her even more roughly than had any other gentleman tonight, with a possessive arm around her waist, and his black domino enveloping her like a sheltering wing. But, truth was, her breath caught in her chest and a tingle of something quite thrilling danced around her heart.

It was hardly proper to tell any of that to him and so she said, striving for affronted virtue, "I can walk on my own, you know."

He paid no heed. He practically carried her along, his arm tight about her so that her toes merely brushed along the floor. She gave up and let him bear her away.

Wolviston felt the tension ease from Clarissa's slight form. Worried, he glanced down at her, but saw only her white mask, and nothing of what emotions might be playing underneath. But she'd had sharp enough words—and elbow—for him. He had to smile. He would stake a year's yield from the home farm that there was not much of anything that could make his fair beauty faint. Not unless she wanted to.

He glanced behind them and saw St. Albans still entangled with the shepherdess he had bribed to provide a distraction.

Next to him, Clarissa pressed into his side, soft and warm, and trembling ever so slightly. She might have an edge to her words, but she had obviously been badly frightened. The impulse—savage and raw—to turn back and deal more directly with St. Albans rose in him. However, he could not do so without giving the man some clue as to Clarissa's identity—and he had already drawn her into enough danger tonight.

Guiding her through the crowd, Wolviston got her to the entrance and out into the cold night air.

On the steps, he stopped to allow his eyes to adjust to the gloom. Flambeaus burned beside the oak double-doors, but the street and surrounding buildings lay in dark shadows. A fine rain had settled over the city, blocking any hint of sky or moonlight.

Next to him, Clarissa shivered, from the cold, or from her experience, he could not tell. He drew her closer, and glanced down at her masked face.

"I should thank you," she said, her voice breathless and husky. She leaned against him, her fingers spread open on his chest. Her perfume teased his senses with a giddy, rose-scented sweetness. Behind the white mask, her eyes seemed so large that they looked almost black and only rimmed by blue edges. He leaned closer to her, drawn by those beguiling eyes, by her scent, by how soft she felt against him.

And then he checked himself.

If she had no mask on, and if they were not standing on a public street, and if he were not really a gentleman, he might have leaned over and kissed her, here with the rain pattering on the cobblestones and the faint noise of the masquerade drifting to them and with the world dark and distant.

But he would have to be a true rogue to take such shameless advantage of her gratitude.

Irritated—with himself for being such a fool as to fall even partially under her spell, and with her for practically inviting his kiss—he looked away, peering

into the dark street. The faint glow of carriage lamps
gave him his direction.

"Come along. You've had a full enough evening.
Lady Havers will see you home."

He took the hand she had pressed against his
chest, but when he tried to pull her with him, he
found her as transportable as one of the columns
that held up the portico around them.

"That is all you want? To send me home? Like
a . . . a child?"

"And what else am I to do?" he asked, his voice
a harsh growl.

Utter disappointment drenched Clarissa's mood
as if he had tossed her out into the rain. This evening had already been awful enough, and now this!
She had thought, after he had rescued her, that at
last he was showing a real interest in her. But now—
after she had done everything but beg for his embrace—he was sending her home.

She wanted to stamp her feet. She wanted to hit
him. She wanted even more for him to kiss her, so
that she would know if there was the promise of
passion between them. What sort of rogue was he
that he did not want even a sample of her lips? She
had been pawed at, leered at, and made love to by
everyone but Wolviston. And, oh, how she wanted
to punish him now for the insult of rejecting her.

Her chin came up. "I suppose your shepherdess
is waiting for you inside?"

His face tightened. "You informed me earlier that
you can walk, so now you may do so to Lady Havers's
coach, or I will carry you."

She tossed her head. "I can manage on my own.

Please don't let me keep you from better amusements."

His grip tightened on her hand until her fingers tingled. "I saw just how well you managed with St. Albans, which is exactly why I will see you safe to your carriage now."

Sliding a sideways glance up at him, she studied the fire in his eyes and the color that slashed across his cheeks. Was that jealousy in his voice? She very much hoped so.

Jerking her fingers away, she folded her hands primly in front of her. "Nonsense. St. Albans, as you call him, was quite charming. He even offered to take me home." She did not add that the home St. Albans had mentioned was his own—Wolviston had no need to know the extent of the danger from which he had saved her.

The next instant Wolviston loomed over. She tried not to step back, but somehow he seemed far more dangerous and imposing than had any other man this evening. His broad shoulders seemed to trap her against the Opera House doors, and the wind whipped his black domino around him as if it were an angry, living thing.

Without another word, he scooped her up.

She ought to have been outraged. Humiliated at the least. Instead, her heart began a new fandango, and that curious tingling shot down to her stomach and curled into a ball of fire. She threw her arm around his neck, but she had no fear that he might drop her. He held her as if he had always done so.

Tight-lipped, he strode to Lady Havers's carriage.

A footman leapt forward to open the coach door and Clarissa found herself tossed inside, onto the red velvet upholstery. She righted herself at once, ripping off her mask. Struggling upright, she watched Wolviston's back as he stalked away into the night.

Jane gawked at her, wide-eyed, and Lady Havers beamed at her. "Why, how nice of Lord Wolviston to carry you across the puddles. Do you know, I vow, I could almost think him a gentleman. Good night, my lord," she called out, leaning forward just before the footman closed the carriage door.

Clarissa pushed at her dampened hair and let out a breath. Slowly, she sank back against the cushions, the fire inside her settling to a warm glow.

"Quite the gentleman," she murmured. Yes, he had proven that he could be. Only how was she to make certain that his reform came attached to his falling in love with her?

Sin was exhausting, Wolviston decided. Not that he had been sinning particularly hard, but after a week of not seeking his bed before dawn, he found it impossible to rise and ride in the morning as had been his previous habit. Seeking out Clarissa at some tame ball or rout began to sound like utter heaven. However, he had a disreputable reputation to build, and he was, after all, here to sow a few damn oats.

He had visited three of the establishments off Covent Garden that Shadwick had named as places where money could buy any pleasure. He had found them amazingly boring. Scantily clad females held a certain obvious allure, but their voluptuous forms seemed overblown, and reminded him how soft and delicate Clarissa had felt pressed against his side.

Their painted faces also seemed overdone when compared with the memory of Clarissa's creamy skin. And their hard eyes left him wondering if Clarissa's eyes were, at that moment, bubbling with some new mischief, or if they were soft and sad with missing him.

Trying to shake off such thoughts, he had wandered through the richly decorated rooms with their gold hangings and lewd paintings. None of it excited him quite as well as did the memory of carrying Clarissa away from the masquerade.

Gaming was even duller. Gentlemen sat in smoky rooms, their coats off—or turned inside out for a change of luck—bands tied around their shirtsleeves to hold up their cuffs, and visors strapped to their foreheads to shade their eyes and expressions from the lamplight over the green baize tables. There was no conversation, just intense concentration on cards or dice or the roulette wheel. Desperation hung in the air like a foul disease, and the few winners would stagger out in the morning with giddy grins, only to be back the next night, hungry for another night's luck.

Wolviston drank a little, played less, and made nodding acquaintances with a few gamesters, who seemed to regard his restraint with wary respect. He watched the deep play with the suspicion that one really must be twenty and green to see any fun in this. He felt as if he were a hundred, and a boring fellow after all. He would almost rather be back with the scantily clad females, overblown figures and all.

He spotted St. Albans at one of the gaming hells, also hanging back and observing the vice around him, like Lucifer in his domain. By the time Wolviston had made his way across the room with the intent of picking an argument that would let him demand satisfaction, St. Albans had vanished. Another time, Wolviston decided, would serve as well to pay back that devil for his licentious treatment of Clarissa.

He spent another hour at the gaming hell, and steadily lost fifty pounds. Restless and not trusting his luck, he decided to leave and perhaps stop in at Lady Perry's musical evening.

An invitation had come his way earlier that week for the affair. He had no acquaintance with Lord Perry or his wife, but Shadwick had assured him that the invitation was indeed meant for him.

"For, m'lord, it is well known that the only thing Lady Perry loves more than scandal is the gentleman who makes it."

Wolviston had his doubts about that, but it was the sort of affair that Clarissa might attend, and it would be interesting to see how she had recovered from her ordeal at the masquerade supper.

Of course, it was only curiosity that prompted such an interest in her. And he had not been intentionally avoiding her this week. Not at all. He had just been making it clear that he was not in the least affected by how she had felt in his arms. He would complete his show of how little she had disturbed him by paying his respects to Lady Perry, and to Lady Havers if she was attending, and then leaving with no more than a nod to Miss Derhurst. If he could get her to glance in his direction, that is.

Lady Perry's house, when he arrived, was still a crush of arriving guests. Rain had the guests scurrying from their carriages to the front steps, dodging puddles, their footmen trying to keep pace with umbrellas that swooped overhead like rather awkward birds of prey. Wolviston found their panic at a bit of wet rather amusing.

A porter hurried forward to open his carriage door, and a liveried footman scurried to take his hat and cape. He shook off the light wetting like a man well accustomed to striding the countryside in far harder downpours.

He had time for no more than a nod from Lord Perry and his wife before they had to turn and pay homage to the Prince Regent as he arrived.

Standing back in deference to royalty, Wolviston was surprised when the Regent paused before him. Corset creaking, the Prince lifted his quizzing glass to study Wolviston's black cravat, and then he muttered before he strolled on, "Hmmm . . . very military. Rather like it."

Amused, Wolviston entered the main room in the tow of the aging Prince.

Decorated with palms and other exotic plants, the room seemed half jungle and half a sea of chairs. A dais had been set up at one end of the rectangular room—for the musical performers, Wolviston judged. He noted a violist talking to a gentleman who stood next to a pianoforte, and decided this must be an interval in the entertainment.

Guests spilled from this room, with its rows of chairs, to the next, some returning with wineglasses and some with plates of food.

He glanced around the milling crowd, feeling as out of place as he had in the gaming den and wondering if this had been such a good idea. Instead of glimpsing Clarissa's laughing face, he found frown-

ing stares cast his direction. Two disapproving dowagers actually lifted their double chins and turned
away from him to cut his acquaintance. Was he developing a reputation? He smiled, a little amused,
but that faint discomfort also deepened inside him
to something that smacked too much of guilt.

Seeing Reggie Preston's sandy hair and immacu-
late figure, Wolviston made his way toward him.
Whispers stirred around him and the crowd seemed
to part before him. The attention left him feeling
as if he were walking about without a stitch of clothing.

"Hallo, Reg. What the devil is amiss with me tonight? Is it the Prince's having noticed me that's
drawing all these stares?"

Reggie regarded his friend, his sandy brows raised
high over amused green eyes. "Have you not heard
the latest? It's going around the room just now that
you might secretly be a royal bastard who is mas-
querading as Lord Wolviston. That nonsense just
started tonight after the Prince Regent took notice
of you. And how'd you get on such friendly terms
with the Prince, old son?"

Wolviston could not decide if he wanted to laugh
or cringe. He opted for what he hoped was a cynical
lift of one eyebrow, and he hoped he had the nerve
to finish this escapade. His reputation seemed to be
acquiring a life of its own.

"I'm royalty, am I? And a bastard? Should I appear
next in a turban so they can think me a sultan?"

"Why not? The truth never matters. Not in Society. But you'd best accustom yourself to being talked
about. The recent spate of rumors, and the fact that

no one really knows anything, has given you an allure, and you've become the topic of the moment."

Wolviston lounged against the wall, his arms crossed. A brazen lady in a clinging red dress fluttered her eyelashes at him over her fan. Her interest flattered, but did not quite entice.

"Do you know, Reggie, I am not certain I like having allure."

Reggie laughed and clapped Wolviston on the shoulder. "Nonsense. Just think of the benefits. You shall now be cut by every tedious Society high-stickler in town. You won't have to avoid matchmaking mamas, because they will avoid you. And the more dashing ladies—well, just take a look at how Lady Firth is eyeing you, old son. If my own past weren't known by one and all, I'd manufacture my own bad reputation as well. It's genius you've hit upon."

Wolviston tried to smile. He tried to ignore the burden of blame that had settled across his shoulders like a yoke at the thought that this scheme had perhaps gone too far. It was just, he told himself, too many years of responsibility which had left him overly sensitive about being anything but a solid, reliable fellow. Still, he wondered if perhaps he had been too rash to invent himself as such a very bad character.

"—and in a year or two, no one will remember anything of your former self and you can reappear as a reformed character," Reggie finished saying, with a flourish of his wineglass.

Letting out a breath, Wolviston straightened. "You're right. I'm seeing trouble in every shadow when I ought to be enjoying myself."

Reggie clapped a hand on his arm and started

guiding him toward the refreshments room. "Too right. Now come and have a glass of—oh, damn, talk about seeing trouble."

With a firm grip on Wolviston's arm, Reggie stopped. "Seems you ain't the only rake, old son, who has caught Miss Derhurst's attention."

"What do you mean?"

Lifting the black ribbon of his quizzing glass, Reggie gestured toward a corner of the room. "Take a look at that! Well, no, not that, that's Lady Cowper flirting with Palmerston again. What I mean is— *that!*"

Glancing in the direction of Reggie's second gesture, Wolviston saw the usual members of Society. Elderly ladies gossiped and compensated for the loss of youth and beauty with too many jewels and too arrogant a manner. Thin and intense gentlemen, their faces gray from overwork, argued politics with other smug, self-satisfied gentlemen. The fashionable few strutted around the room, displaying the cut of their clothes, and those less fashionable whispered cutting remarks about them.

Wolviston was amazed to realized that in less than a month, he found he knew this world so well.

And then he glimpsed her.

She had been hidden from his view by the Prince Regent, who was now moving his bulky figure away. Clarissa, made even more beautiful by the flush on her cheeks, took his eye and his breath.

She wore a dress of gold and white, with blue flowers embroidered about the hem and the close-fitting bodice. Her lack of jewelry made every other woman seem overdressed. Gold curls flashed like fresh-minted guinea coins. Her eyes sparkled. She looked,

Wolviston judged, like a woman who had just been flattered extravagantly—and perhaps touched a little too intimately. Knowing the Regent's reputation with attractive women, Wolviston judged both to be the case.

"Did you know the Prince would be here tonight?" Wolviston asked, scowling and glaring after the Regent's departing form. Lord, it would not do for Clarissa to become too intimate with the Regent. The Prince was known to run with a disreputable set—men all too eager to press their attentions on any desirable lady, whether she was unmarried or not.

Reggie let out a frustrated breath and then said, "It ain't the Prince that's the problem. It's him."

Puzzled, Wolviston glanced at his friend, wondering just how much burgundy Reggie had put away this evening, and then he glanced back at Clarissa and his blood chilled.

There, next to Clarissa, smiling at her and holding her hand, stood the Earl of St. Albans.

Six

Clarissa tried to keep her smile in place, but her head swam, and not from the heat of the room. She kept telling herself that St. Albans could not have recognized her. He could not know that she was the lady he had tried to unmask at the Opera House. She had nothing to fear. Only she could not stop her pulse from hammering in her throat, and she could not do anything about the weight of dread that lay in her stomach.

She also could not forget how the Earl of St. Albans had watched her as Lady Perry had presented the Prince Regent and then himself to her. Polite manners dictated that she curtsy deeply to the Prince, and every instinct in her urged her to act as if she had never met the Earl.

The Regent had pinched her chin and leaned closer, his corset creaking and his breath reeking of brandy, to utter lavish compliments that she had barely heard. He had looked so old, with tired eyes and fleshy cheeks, that he had reminded her of one of her least favorite great-uncles. He had not seemed at all like the prince in the stories that her mother had once told her about when she had met this first gentleman of Europe.

St. Albans was another matter.

After the Prince moved on, St. Albans remained beside her, a mocking smile hovering on his lips, and a knowing look in his eyes that left her fiddling nervously with her fan.

"I vow we have met before, have we not, Miss Derhurst?" St. Albans said, a fashionable drawl in his voice.

She raised her eyebrows. "I would remember if we had been formally introduced."

His smile widened. "Ah, but you have such distinctive golden hair—like ripe wheat in a summer sun."

Her temper and her lips thinned at his obvious teasing, but she kept her voice determinedly good-natured. "The normal list is to start with my eyes. Some compared them to sapphires, but most prefer the conventional pools of spring water. You should then progress to my complexion, which most gentlemen seem to liken to that of an angel's. I must assume they refer to the paintings of angels, since first-hand heavenly introductions are rather hard to come by these days. Then you may compliment my hair. But I urge you to strive for a little more originality than to compare my hair to a crop, or to say that we must have met before."

He laughed, his face momentarily transformed by good humor, and for an instant Clarissa found herself smiling along with him. But then the sharpness in his expression returned, and so did her wariness.

"Ah, my sweet mystery, you add spice to what has become a stale and predictable world. Come, say you forgive me for my poor behavior the other night."

Still a little angry with him, she started to answer that she did not forgive him, but then she caught herself. To say anything would be to admit that she had been at the Opera House the other evening. And Lady Havers had already warned of the importance of maintaining a spotless reputation.

She widened her eyes with false innocence. "I cannot forgive an offense whose cause I do not recognize. Perhaps you should seek out the lady whom you believe you have wronged?"

"Oh, I have sought her. She so interested me that I have been driven to attend such dull affairs as these to find her. And what is my reward but to be disclaimed?"

She could not help but be flattered. An earl, a friend of the Prince Regent, a known rake, and he had sought out her company. However, when her stare met his cool, green eyes, he smiled at her, but it was a secret, knowing smile. She disliked that smile. It said that he had seen through her disguise of the other evening, and that he was intent on teasing her with his knowledge.

She decided that all he really wanted was to goad an unguarded admission that she had been at the masquerade, and so she said, "Well, if you find the entertainment here so little to your taste, perhaps you should go and seek better amusements."

He stepped closer. "I have found all the amusement I need for the moment."

Something in his glance—a predatory intensity—sent a jolt of alarm through her. She glanced around, seeking the comforting presence of Jane, or Lady Havers, or even Reggie Preston. Instead, Wolviston loomed out of the crowd, dressed in severe black, his gray eyes storming.

Her heart gave a small jump. She took a breath

to steady herself, and then snapped open her fan to cool her face and slow her pulse.

Wolviston stopped before her and gave a small bow. "Good evening, Miss Derhurst." He glanced at St. Albans and said nothing—an intentional slight that had the Earl's eyes narrowing.

Clarissa stepped between them at once. It was no part of her plans to have these two acting like bulls thrown into the same pasture—with her as the complaisant, bystanding cow.

"Lord St. Albans, may I present to you Viscount Wolviston. My Lord Wolviston, this is. . . ."

"Simon Winters, Earl of St. Albans, Baron Winters, and known by a few other trifling titles," St. Albans said with a slight, mocking bow.

"And some of them, no doubt, cannot be used in mixed company," Wolviston muttered. He had the satisfaction of watching St. Albans's mouth tighten with annoyance.

St. Albans turned to Clarissa. "You must excuse me. The company has suddenly become rather vulgar. But now that I have found you, I intend that we shall meet again."

With a smile, Clarissa gave him her gloved hand. St. Albans pressed her fingers, then, after glancing at Wolviston, he kissed her fingertips and took his leave.

She turned a blameless face to Wolviston's glowering one, delighted that St. Albans's unnerving attentions had produced one satisfactory result. They had made Wolviston jealous.

"I should have thought you'd had enough of St. Albans's company the other evening," Wolviston said, his voice low.

She certainly had, and she had not the least intention of admitting it. Wolviston did deserve just a little punishment for neglecting her these past few days.

Opening her fan, she began to ply it, as if bored. "It is quite a wonderful thing to find a gentleman so attentive as the Earl of St. Albans."

Wolviston's mouth turned down and she knew she had scored a hit. However, her knowledge of her Uncle Andrew had taught her one wisdom—that of not pushing a man too far.

So she laid her hand on Wolivston's arm and offered up one of her prettiest smiles. "I do believe the music is about to begin again. Would you be so kind as to take me back to where my godmama has seats? It is just over by the door, near the front there."

He did not refuse her request, but strode to Lady Havers's side, making no attempt to shorten his step for her. She had to hurry along as he led her through the rows of chairs toward where Lady Havers sat with Jane Preston. He scowled, and she wondered if he wanted to be rid of her. She racked her mind for some way to make him stay.

Lady Havers offered her a solution.

Glancing up as they approached, Lady Havers smiled and invited Wolviston to sit with them. Clarissa added her most charming, inviting smile to that lady's request.

It had not been Wolviston's intent to stay. He wanted only to leave this flirtatious baggage of a girl with her godmother. Here she was encouraging St. Albans's interest, and then turning around to try her smiles out on the next man who strode up to her! And, damn, but the room seemed far too warm when she did smile up at him in just that fashion, her eyes glowing with humor and that luscious mouth curving into a soft bow.

Uneasy from that smile of hers, he started to form some excuse, but the words tangled in a suddenly sluggish brain. Why did she have to look up at him with eyes so indecently blue?

Then the hairs on the back of his neck tingled. A glance up and across the room showed St. Albans watching them, an eager interest in his expression. That tore it. He was not about to step aside and leave St. Albans an opening for a return.

With a gracious smile and bow, Wolviston accepted the lady's offer and made himself as comfortable as he could in the hard, narrow chairs that Lady Perry had set out for her guests. Lady Havers seemed delighted. Miss Preston managed a shy smile. And as the quartette returned to the dais, Clarissa turned not toward him, but toward the musicians.

Frowning, Wolviston folded his arms. He had never had any great fondness for music and did not expect much from this evening, other than that he was keeping St. Albans away from Clarissa and Jane Preston. He was surprised, however, and not by the music.

The quartette performed several tunes, lively things with nice enough melodies. Wolviston could only be glad they were short pieces. Then an exotic lady, with a curvaceous figure and a weight of diamonds slung about her neck, came forward. Her voice—deeper than most—pleased his ear, and while she sang, accompanied by a pianoforte, Wolviston's enjoyment shifted to observing the ladies next to him.

Lady Havers sat gossiping with her friends, whispering and ignoring the entertainment, except to applaud when required. Next to her, Jane Preston listened with such an empty look in her eyes that Wolviston knew her mind had wandered miles away. But Clarissa . . . Clarissa was different.

She did not tap her fan, nor did her head sway in exaggerated and artificial appreciation.

Utterly still, she leaned forward slightly in her seat. Her eyes drifted closed, almost as if she were willing herself into the music.

He watched, fascinated by the transformation. Gone were the coquettish glances and the practiced pouts and poses. The music seemed to strip away her pretenses, leaving behind a startling maturity. She was a beauty now—but in a few years, he saw that she could become something far more extraordinary.

He studied the lines of her face, the strong curve of jaw that tapered to the rounded chin. The straight nose. The elegant line of her cheek. The beauty would fade. But the intensity inside her, the vitality behind that glowing skin, the force of personality that shone from her eyes, that inner fire burned so bright that no decay could dim its luminescence.

Yes, she could become something far more than a spoilt beauty.

She could become a woman of soul-searing passion.

And he was drawn to that still-budding woman as he had been to no others.

Ah, what would it be like to see that incandescence become a deeper fire? And to feel it burn against his own skin? Had she—under that spoilt beauty—a heart to awaken as well?

All too soon, the soprano finished her final aria— something in Italian that he found incomprehensible. Clarissa let out a deep sigh, then opened her eyes and applauded. The rapture on her face still hovered close, in the radiance of her skin and the sweet lift at the corner of her mouth where the faintest dimple hovered.

As the singer stepped from the dais to be introduced to the Prince and other notables, Clarissa turned to Wolviston, her eyes glowing. "Was she not marvelous? Oh, how I wish I had such a voice."

He smiled at her. "I thought every young lady could sing."

She made a face. "According to my uncle, I have a tolerable voice. And he, according to my mother, was once a fine musician before he joined the army. So he would know. Do you like music?"

The question came out artless and for once he found himself answering her just as honestly. "My mother adores sad ballads of love in which someone inevitably dies, so I cannot claim any particular fondness, no."

Some of the glow left her face and he could have kicked himself for dampening her pleasure with the lack of his own. So he added, "But I think I might like it more if I knew more about it."

Her face brightened and she began to chatter on about composers, and voice qualities, and Italian terms that left his head spinning. He listened, however, still surprised by this new aspect to her. He had thought her quite as shallow as Lady Havers, an indulged and willful child. Now he began to wonder just what else lay behind that mask of beauty.

With a few questions, he began to draw her out about her family. Her father had died several years ago, and from the way she shied away from the topic, it seemed as if perhaps she was still not recovered from that loss. He certainly understood the urge to protect such wounds. Her mother sounded almost as silly a woman as Lady Havers, and listening to what Clarissa said, he judged her to be a woman more consumed by her own needs than those of her daughter.

As to the uncle and guardian—Lord Rothe—Wolviston could not make out if the man was as much an ogre as the picture Clarissa seemed inclined to paint. Or perhaps he was simply a man trying to cope with this girl who seemed bent upon growing up all too fast. Clarissa certainly seemed to relish stories of her Uncle Andrew's harsh opinions and his autocratic ways, but Wolviston also heard a touch of pride in her voice when she spoke of him.

"But my aunt—that is, Lady Rothe—she has a lovely voice. A true contralto. Far better than my own, although I can never get her to own to it. I do so miss hearing her sing little Sophie to sleep. She is my niece, and an utterly adorable baby. I quite see why Aunt Maeve so wanted another one like her as soon as possible. I certainly should have. Although I do think it was awful of Uncle Andrew to get her with child right when she was to bring me to London, but Aunt Maeve said it was as much her fault as his."

Wolviston smiled, amused at this indiscreet admission. "And was it?"

"Well, yes, I supposed it must be. Theirs was a love match, although they probably would not have married at all if I had not stepped in to give them a push. Honestly, it does amaze me how people can refuse utterly the promptings of their own hearts."

"But you know your heart, Miss Derhurst?"

She stared at him, her eyes wide. "Of course I do. I will know the instant I fall in love with the man whom I will marry and love forever."

Her face softened and he almost made the mistake of believing her. But then he remembered her scorn in the garden for men who lived in the country, and who did not have scandalous pasts. Men such as him.

How could she ever really love any man when she was so enamored with an illusion?

"So you'll know all that? How amazing," he said, letting the scorn drip into his voice. "And you will not allow any rational thoughts to influence your heart? You will love this gentleman no matter what his past, and no matter what the future may bring?"

Eyebrows raised, she gave him a belligerent stare. "True love does not judge. It simply is."

"Perhaps I shall be able to remind you of these words someday, Miss Derhurst."

Clarissa shivered at the cold contempt in his voice. She did not understand what had just happened. Did he not believe her that she might be able to love him, no matter what his past?

Self-conscious, she looked away and saw St. Albans watching. Her stomach knotted as St. Albans smiled, bowed, and then turned away. She glanced down at her hands and saw that they were wrapped tightly around her fan.

Oh, where had she gotten herself? She had wanted one rake—one gentleman she could reform and love. Only now she had two, it seemed, as well as a tight ache in her chest and a feeling as if she were being swept out to sea by currents she could not see or control.

None of this was going as planned. It had seemed so straightforward when she and Jane used to stay up nights, talking about their London season and about the bold, romantic rakes who would sweep them off their feet.

She glanced up at Wolviston. He had on his ironic face, his emotions masked again by a skeptical look in those flat, gray eyes and a polite smile that said nothing to her. The barriers had risen, invisible but unassailable.

Trying not to scowl, she thought about accidentally treading on his foot. She would rather have anger from him than this distant stranger. But she tried to be patient. Had she set off his defenses with the mention of children? Oh, dear, it would not do if he did not want children, for she wanted dozens. Three at least. She had been an only child herself and she wanted her own children to have plenty of playmates.

Oh, dear, what if it is my children he doesn't want? she thought, worry nibbling at her confidence.

But then Lady Havers was standing and shaking out her skirts and saying they must go. Clarissa had to stand and smile and give Wolviston her hand. He did no more than bow over it and turn away, heading for the door, his stride purposeful.

Clarissa watched him, her enjoyment of the evening gone. With a deep sigh, she wondered if perhaps she was trying to entice the wrong rake into reforming.

"You're going to end up married to her if you're not careful."

A little shocked, Wolviston turned away from the prime bit of muslin he had been admiring in Mrs. Beale's establishment in Soho Square off Oxford Street. Discreet, tastefully decorated in silk hangings of Wedgwood blue and cream, the house offered scantily clad women who could provide witty conversation, or a good deal more, as a gentleman preferred.

Wolviston had dragged Reggie with him, determined to enjoy himself, to live it up a little, and to put images of golden hair and a pouting smile out of his mind. It was raining tonight, and Wolviston's mood was as dark as the skies overhead.

"Marry her? I haven't even met her." Wolviston indicated the pretty brunette he had been admiring.

Reggie glanced at her and then scowled. "Not her. The Derhurst. I heard about your rescue of her last week. Oh, stop looking so thunderous. It's not common gossip. Jane told me about the masquerade. And you can't go around rescuing ladies without their getting ideas about it."

Wolviston lounged back in his chair. The brunette found another gentleman, ready to pay for more than a view of her charms, and she left the room on his arm. Wolviston turned his attention to another women, this one a redhead who smiled and posed and cast sly glances at him.

"Reggie, a man would have to be a raving bedlamite to allow a female such as Clarissa, with her whims and willful ways, a free hand with his life. I am only out to give her a lesson about judging others. And I am nowhere near ready to shackle myself down to a wife!"

And that is the way it will damn well remain, he told

himself. He had the firm suspicion that Clarissa would be ready to claw his eyes out if he now told her that he had been leading her down the garden path with his stories of being a rake.

"That's what you say now. But mark my words. You're in dangerous waters, old son. First a rescue. Soon they're invading your dreams, and then they steal your freedom." Reggie stared into his empty brandy glass.

Shifting in his seat, Wolviston gave Reggie an irritable stare and said, "You sound as if you're speaking from experience."

Reggie glowered back. "I am damn well not."

A grin stole into Wolviston. "Be damned if you aren't. Who is it? What female's caught your heart?"

"No one," Reggie growled. "Now, I thought we came out to enjoy ourselves. This place is amazingly flat. Don't know why your man recommended it for sinful amusements."

Wolviston let his stare slide across the room. All seemed discreet and innocent. Almost. He had the same sense as at the masquerade that less tame amusements could be had behind closed curtains. For the right price.

He drank off his brandy, however, and complied with Reggie's wish. For while Mrs. Beale's girls were pretty—and he could certainly see enough of them to judge all their charms—he kept thinking of blue eyes that turned indigo with anger, and one particular set of pouting lips.

I have to get that female out of my mind.

"What's that you said?" Reggie asked.

"Nothing, Reggie. Now, let's go find a gaming hell to take some of our money."

The rain pelted from the sky, drenching and cold with a bite of winter still in its gusting. Not a carriage for hire could be found, so they walked down the street to a cozy private club. Leaving their capes and wet hats with the porter, they were ushered into the quiet, dim depths of The Key in Chandros Street.

Wolviston won. But Reggie steadily drank and lost.

Not great sums. Wolviston kept enough wits, and an always full glass of brandy at his side, so that he seemed to be drinking when he was doing no more than nursing one glass through an evening. He also kept an eye on his friend, and when Reggie turned obstinate, trying to win his lost money back, Wolviston decided it was time for them to find their beds.

He got Reggie as far as the front entrance when the door from the main hall opened and in stepped St. Albans.

Dressed in black and silver, the man looked as fresh as if he had just stepped from his chambers, instead of having been out more than half the night. Wolviston became aware of the stubble on his cheeks, the loose cravat around his neck, and the wrinkles in his coat.

St. Albans cast a scornful glance at Reggie's tottering state, and then turned to Wolviston, one eyebrow raised. "I had thought this to be a select club."

Wolviston's fingers tightened on Reggie's arms, so much so that Reggie jerked upright.

"Whass wrong?" He leaned forward in Wolviston's grip, peering at St. Albans. "Oh . . . is you, Sunt Albaaans," he slurred. "'m not so drunk I don't know you. Am I, Evan?"

Turning, Reggie started to slide to the floor. Wolviston backed him to a chair so that Reggie sat down instead of falling down. Then Wolviston turned back to St. Albans.

"Do you know, St. Albans, I dislike how you always seem to be stepping into my path."

For a moment, St. Albans stared at him, his eyes cold. Then his mouth quirked. "It seems we share that in common, among other things."

"I have nothing to share with you, sir."

St. Albans kept smiling, but now it was only a slight curve of his lips; his eyes turned as cold as moss on granite. "But we are men of the world, are we not? Both vice hardened. Both interested in the same thing—in virtue. They say it is its own reward. And certainly virtue often does leave the ladies so obligingly ignorant, does it not?"

Wolviston's jaw clenched and his hands fisted. Still, he checked himself. If he struck that smirk from the man's face there might be those who would remember that both he and St. Albans had both shown interest in Miss Derhurst. He had been the one to put her into St. Albans's path by inviting her to that damned masquerade. He could not afford to endanger her reputation by dragging her name into a gaming hell.

So he relaxed his hands and smiled. Pleasantly, he hoped. "Actually, I find that virtue is often dull as the grave." And that was the utter truth.

St. Albans's eyebrows arched with surprise. "I would not have thought you found it so earlier this evening. But there was so much more than virtue to be interested in, was there not? Do you know, ordinarily I do not believe in hunting another man's territory. But I find I cannot allow you to be unchallenged for this particular vixen we've set up a halloo after."

"Go to hell."

St. Albans's smile widened. "Oh, I shall in due time. And probably all that much faster for what I plan for that fair-haired vixen who has earned our interest."

That cut it. Fist bunching, Wolviston started to growl out a low-voiced threat to St. Albans about the unhealthy prospects awaiting the man should he continue to show interest in Miss Derhurst. However, Reggie's cheerful cry stopped him cold.

"David! Peter! Look, Evan! Look who's here!"

Wolviston glanced up and then reeled as if he'd been hit by an invisible fist. There in the hallway entrance to the gaming hell stood two youths. Their faces bore the same stamp of high cheekbones, tousled golden-blond hair, and dark eyes. Both were tall, well-built young men, but the gentleman on the left carried the advantage of two more inches in height, while the other owned a sweetness in his face that would someday soon have the women sighing over him.

They had adopted fashionable extremes—the new Russian trousers that bagged about their ankles like loose canvas sails, and coats that nipped in tight at the waist and puffed up at the shoulders. The taller of the two sported a striped waistcoat, while his companion flourished a purple cravat.

They looked primed for a lark, and Wolviston knew that look well.

He had seen it in their faces when they had chopped down his mother's favorite apple tree to make a Viking longboat. He had seen it the day they had come home covered in mud after betting on who could ride Farmer Milton's best sow.

Just now his two younger brothers looked shame-faced and guilty as only schoolboys caught in sin could.

"Excuse me," Wolviston muttered, and started for the entrance, pausing only long enough to haul Reggie to his feet before he forcefully guided his friend and his brothers into the entrance hall.

St. Albans watched as Wolviston, his drunken friend in tow, descended on two green-faced youths like an avenging angel about to banish them from paradise. About all Wolviston lacked was a suitably flaming sword, he thought, his mouth twisting.

And then he frowned.

An angel indeed. First so protective of the pretty Derhurst. Now he seemed to have taken up bear-leading these youths. Quite noble for a man whose reputation was supposed to be one of a hell-raiser and a womanizer.

St. Albans studied the tableau a moment, his antipathy for Wolviston growing. Reggie Preston swayed and grinned like the drunken fool he was. The youths—David and Peter, good Biblical names—began to look sullen and cowed, and rather familiar, with their strong noses and lean faces. But, no, he had not heard any mention of brothers. Cousins perhaps? Certainly not bastard children, for Wolviston was too young to have sons who looked of an age to be at university.

Wolviston herded them out the door with the efficiency that he had used on the charming Miss Derhurst, and left St. Albans in a sour mood.

He loathed men who pretended that virtue existed in this world. And this latent nobility in Wolviston brought out the urge to see it revealed for the sham it was.

And he thought he knew the best way to do that.

He had been quite honest tonight. He normally did not like to poach on another man's territory. Not from any virtuous impulse, of course, but because most men had such low standards for true female beauty.

The Derhurst, however, was something different. He had known it the instant he had seen her at that masked dinner. She had shimmered like a diamond set among tawdry paste gems, and tonight she had shown glimpses of something far more rare—originality.

Still, the inopportune Wolviston had a point—virtue could be dull. And St. Albans knew himself well enough to know that while La Derhurst attracted him now, it was unlikely to last. It never did. Naked and in bed, all women seemed the same.

Ah, but how much more amusing would the game be with La Derhurst if Wolviston was also competing for the fair prize?

It would be a heartless thing to court Miss Derhurst for no better reason than to see what trouble he might cause between her and Wolviston. But it would be vastly entertaining.

Seven

Wolviston pushed away his uneaten cold beef and took up his coffee. A glance at the rosewood clock on the mantel showed ten minutes before ten. Ten minutes before his brothers were due to arrive with an explanation of why they were in London, not Cambridge. Ten minutes for him to stop feeling guilty, as if they had been the ones to catch him in devilment.

Which they had been.

Burdened with a drunken Reggie, and seeing that both the boys were the worse for drink themselves, he had sent them off to their lodgings, ordering them to present themselves at his Albany residence on the morrow at the stroke of ten. It had seemed a reasonable idea to allow them to anticipate a dressing down. But he had forgotten how much he dreaded these damn interviews himself.

He had always felt like such a humbug, trying to discipline them when half the time he had been envious of their freedom. And how could he fault them for wanting some fun? He had come to London with the same intent. It was worse now that he honestly was the one who was up to mischief, pretending to be a rake. Lord, how could he ever hope to command their respect again if they learned about his pretense?

"Not hungry, m'lord?"

Wolviston glanced up into Shadwick's impassive face. "A gallows-bait would have more appetite on the morn before he hangs. Damn if I know what I'm going to say to my brothers when they show themselves. I fear I make a poor substitute for a father, Shadwick."

The valet began to remove the china from the round table set up in the main parlor, arranging it on a black lacquered butler's tray. "Then perhaps, m'lord, you should strive simply to be their brother."

Wolviston let out a sigh. Excellent advice if he knew how to use it. The boys had been ten and nine when their father's accident had knocked the family to pieces. It might have been easier if there had not been such a gulf in ages between himself and the boys. Or if his mother had not been prone to worry herself into fits over every little thing.

But he could hardly fault her for her deep concern. There had been two children between him and his brothers—both girls—who had not survived their infancy, and it had left their mother more protective of the boys than was good for them. He had become both a shield between the boys and their mother's smothering affection, and the person who'd had to offer discipline and guidance.

Had he failed at it all?

Rising, Wolviston took his coffee cup with him to the window that overlooked the courtyard, which opened out onto Piccadilly. Clouds chased across an uncertain sky, and it looked as if it might rain again later in the day. Below the Albany, a trio of gentlemen, arms linked, strode away from the building. Further out, on Piccadilly itself, Wolviston glimpsed a baker passing, carrying fresh bread in wide, woven baskets slung over his arms. He saw nothing of a pair of young gentlemen got up in fashionable clothing.

Turning back to his valet, he asked, "What would you do, Shadwick, if your younger brothers turned up in town, prime for any lark? Would you send them home, or let them stay and enjoy their youth?"

Tray in hand, Shadwick straightened, his face impassive. "That would be difficult for me to say, m'lord, as I am the youngest in my family."

Wolviston raised an eyebrow. "That is not very helpful."

"I beg your pardon, m'lord. But I can tell you from the other end of it that it was always easier to go to an older brother with my problems than it was to go to my father. One does so hate to disappoint a father, or a father figure. Particularly if he seems so formidably capable himself."

Wolviston gave a wry smile. "I doubt my brothers think me all that capable when I've never done anything much."

"That, m'lord, is a matter of perspective. And the view from ten years younger can be rather awe inspiring."

Frowning, Wolviston mulled these words over as Shadwick bowed himself from the room. Did his brothers find him awe inspiring? In fact, had he made himself into a rather dreadful fellow? A man too harsh with them, and perhaps too quick to quell their high spirits? The question troubled him, and left him even more uncertain what he ought to do with them.

Five minutes later, he was still frowning at his coffee, cold now in its china cup, when Shadwick ushered in his brothers.

Wolviston put down his coffee and looked David and Peter over with fresh eyes. Did they really find him all that intimidating?

They had left off their fashionable attire. Both now wore familiar riding breeches and tan-topped riding boots, with conservative double-breasted brown coats. Tan waistcoats peeked out from under their buttoned coats.

David sported a struggling pair of side whiskers— wispy blond growth that curled around his ears. And Peter, the younger by a year, filled out the shoulders of his coat in a startling new way. Their faces had a tight, set look, and the gazes from two pairs of brown eyes had a distressing tendency to shy away from Wolviston.

David, coloring slightly under his older brother's scrutiny, shuffled an awkward bow. "You wanted to see us, sir?"

Wolviston winced. Since when had he become *sir*? He gestured to a pair of leather chairs and seated himself on the sofa, laying an arm across the back of it. "I vow, I won't be able to be seen anywhere with the two of you looking such rustics as you do now."

Peter's face brightened. "You aren't sending us home?"

"That remains to be seen. By the way, I assume there is some reason for your absence from university with Easter Term close to beginning?"

"I only wanted some honey for my tea," David said, a defiant look in his eyes as if he expected instant condemnation.

"And everything would have been fine if the vicar hadn't been walking past when David set the hive on fire," Peter added, his voice anxious.

Wolviston had to smooth the smile off his face with one hand. It really would not do to be encouraging them, but it was a relief to hear it was some boyish prank—not serious trouble—that had caused what must be a temporary suspension.

He gestured again to the chairs. "You had better sit down. This bodes to be a long story."

Peter took the lead in telling, his gestures growing more animated as he spoke. His hair—once golden and now darkening like David's—fell forward as he spoke, and he started to look more like the boy that Wolviston had always known.

Still sullen, David inserted rather cryptic comments about good intentions and vicars who ought to be in bed, which led Wolviston to believe he was smarting from an excess of guilt.

It seemed that, during a night of revels, David had acquired a craving for honey. And the nearest vicar raised bees. However, instead of subduing the bees with smoke—as they had been shown one summer at Wolviston Abbey—they managed to light a blaze that had melted a good number of hives. The fire had roused the vicar, a good deal of the university, and some rather irate bees.

Numerous stings later, the end result had been that the two Fortesque boys had been rusticated for the last part of Lent Term. And they had been fined for the cost of replacing the vicar's hives.

"So you thought you'd try your luck at winning the cost of the fine?" Wolviston said, already guessing the line of thought that had led his brothers to a London gaming hell.

David's chin lifted. "We did, sir."

"Plus a hundred pounds more the first night," Peter added.

"Ah, I see now where the new clothes came from. And how much did you subsequently lose?"

Red flooded up David's neck and into his cheeks. He and Peter exchanged a look that spoke of shared disaster and a common bond. Wolviston saw that look and a pang of envy twisted inside him. He had always been thankful that they had each other. Now he wished he'd had more of their friendship as well.

Shifting in his seat, Wolviston waved away the matter of lost money. "You can draw on next quarter's allowance if you need. Just remember, that's the sort of place where a new face always wins. And they make it their business to make it sinfully easy to lose after that."

Peter frowned. "Then what were you do—owww!"

An elbow into his ribs silenced Peter, and he glared at David, who stared ahead as if nothing had happened.

Wolviston glanced from one brother to the other, and then let the moment pass. His affairs were no concern of his brothers—while theirs were very much his. Standing, he strode to the window, his hands folded behind his back. Then he turned and faced his brothers.

"I ought to order you home until the start of next term."

"Oh, please, Evan," Peter protested. "You know

Mother. She'll have us stripped and searched for bee stings, and then she'll have one of her dashed concoctions smothered over us. What was it the last time we came home soaked from shooting?"

"Onions on our ears and mustard on our chests," David muttered, sounding resigned to a fate worse than death.

"That might be a suitable punishment," Wolviston said.

The boys hung their heads and said nothing.

In the room, the clock ticked steadily. The cry of "Strawberries, scarlet strawberries!" carried into the room from a vendor walking the courtyard below.

Suddenly, David rose up, fists clenched, his chin jutting forward. "Damn it, Evan. Just because you never had any fun, is it any reason to deny us a chance to live a little?"

His words had spilled out hot and fast, and now he stared at Wolviston, his eyes growing large, as if he had shocked himself with this outburst. His stare fell to the carpet, and head down, he muttered an apology.

With his face burning as if he had been slapped, Wolviston stared at his brothers. Good god, had he perhaps been as overzealous in his protection of the boys as his mother? Did they feel so confined by him that they never would have told him about this London escapade if he had not run across them?

Frowning, he asked, "Where do you have lodgings?"

Peter wet his lips and then said, "The White Horse in Fetter Lane. It's where the mail coach from Cambridge left us."

Wolviston knew London well enough now to recognize that the inn, located near Temple Garden, just east of Lincoln Inn, was an area with cheap establishments and dubious respectability. It was, however, well enough for two young men on their own.

"And if you were to stay in London, what would you do with your time?"

David's head lifted a fraction. He eyed his older brother warily, his brown eyes still dark and troubled. "We just want to see something of the world."

Peter nodded. "Like Astley's performing equestrians—is it true, Evan, that the girls really do ride horses naked?"

"Don't be stupid—Evan wouldn't know that," David said, scornful of his brother's ignorance. And then he colored under Wolviston's steady regard. "I mean, not the sort of place you'd go, now is it?"

"No, it's far too dashing for me. I usually stay home with a book and sit beside the fire to warm my arthritic hips."

David gave his younger brother a nod, as if to say, *see what I mean?*

Goaded, Wolviston told them, "It may come as a shock, but I actually have something of a reputation in town."

"As what?" Peter asked.

David cuffed his brother. "You idiot. Don't you remember hearing the rumors? He's courting that Derhurst girl."

Wolviston stiffened. His words came out sharp and clear. "Just what did you hear?"

The brothers exchanged worried glances. Then David spoke up. "Uh . . . just some mention of a bet. About who would snare this Miss Derhurst first, you or some fellow named St. Albans."

Wolviston swore to himself, and put up a hand to rub the furrow between his eyes. Oh, hell. He had not meant to endanger Clarissa's reputation by making up a bad one for himself. But he had indeed started this deception, so it would be up to him to end it. And it looked as if he had best do so soon. Before any serious trouble came of it. Well, he had faced unpleasant tasks before—and he was damn tired of them.

But he would end it.

"Never mind about Miss Derhurst," he said. "However, you will tell me if you hear her name mentioned again with anything less than respect and honor."

The two brothers exchanged a rather surprised look, and Peter sat forward as if he wanted to ask other questions. But Wolviston found himself curiously reluctant to speak of her further. It was not as if there was anything else to say, after all. She was nothing to him. The sting of her scorn had long since lessened and he really could not blame her for how tangled everything had become.

He also had two other worries just now, who sat before him, waiting for his judgment.

With one eyebrow lifted, he regarded his brothers. "If you were to stay, do you think you could manage to keep out of the worst sorts of trouble until it is time for your return to Cambridge and your studies?"

David stared at him, his mouth falling open, and Peter stood up, grinning. "Do you mean it, sir? We may stay?"

"If you stop calling me 'sir,' and if you can show me you actually do know how to behave in front of

Society, then, yes, you can. But only until the start of next term, mind you."

For the first time David grinned, and a shade of boyish grace that Wolviston recognized slipped back into the young man he was becoming. "Oh, we'll not get into any trouble, Evan. I vow, we won't."

Wolviston folded his arms. Coming from someone who had recently set fire to a vicar's beehives, that promise carried dubious weight. But then he looked at the two eager faces turned up to his, and he knew that he could not have sent them home. Not without creating an even deeper gulf between himself and them.

But a harder task than that of keeping them out of trouble now lay before him. He had to find a way to tell Clarissa that he really wasn't a rake at all. And the thought of doing that made him wish that someone would just send him home and out of harm's way.

Another stem snapped in Clarissa's hands and she scowled at the carnation as if it were its fault for breaking.

"Are you arranging or murdering those poor flowers?" Jane asked.

Jane sat curled up on a chair in Lady Havers's conservatory, a paisley shawl loose across her elbows and half obscuring her green morning dress. A book lay neglected on her lap as she watched Clarissa, who stood before a long, wooden table strewn with flowers. Clipping shears lay abandoned beside one of the four empty Chinese vases arranged on the table. One of the vases stood before Clarissa, half full of limp flowers, which looked as if they had been exhausted by their ordeal.

The glass conservatory doors had been folded back, allowing full access from the house to the greenroom, in which Lord Havers, before his death, had installed steam heating to keep plants alive year round. Now forced bulbs blossomed, dotting the room with yellows and pale blues; pink and white carnations wove their spicy aroma into the air, and red roses bloomed as if it were full summer.

Clarissa, dressed in a high-necked blue gown, looked as hot and bothered as if it were indeed summer already, although it was only just April. Her curls tumbled around her face, held back by a patterned scarf that she had used to hastily tie them up. Heat and exasperation flushed her cheeks, and she glared at the flowers as if she would pick them up and thrash them to their doom on the edge of the table.

She had been arranging flowers for Lady Havers's public rooms. Her ladyship was having a small dinner with impromptu dancing tomorrow night—only a hundred and twenty close friends had been invited. Flowers had also been ordered, but her ladyship had told Clarissa, "My dear, the personal touch is always the most admired, so you must do the flowers for the hall and dining room yourself."

Clarissa knew quite well that the event—and the demonstration of demure flower arranging skills— were all part of her ladyship's plans to quell recent rumors circulating over the past week or so about Clarissa's having attracted not one, but two rakes. She had heard the whispers that no decent young lady attracted such attention, unless she had done something to entice such rogues to her.

She had shrugged off the rumors. They stung, but she had long ago developed her own armor against the jealous words that often came at her because of her looks.

Dealing with recalcitrant flowers was a much harder task.

Staring at the third stem she had snapped in as many minutes, Clarissa let out a frustrated sigh. "They simply won't go where I want them to!"

Rising, Jane came over and took up a yet unbroken lily from the table. "Rather a lot like gentlemen, aren't they?"

Clarissa frowned for a moment, and then could not resist Jane's smile. "I am so ungrateful, I know."

"Yes, you are. This week alone you have had yellow roses from Lord St. Albans, violets from Lord Morrow, and lilacs from Sir Anthony, as well as lilies cut by the gardener just for you."

Wrinkling her nose, Clarissa said, "I know I should be flattered and pleased."

"Yes, you ought to be! I've not seen so much as a posy from any gentleman."

"Oh, Jane, I wish I could give them all to you—the gentlemen and their flowers, and their flattery, and their fawning."

Jane pulled a wry face. "And I know how happy you would be if you went two days without someone dancing attendance on you. I remember what you were like that year we were both first at school."

The color deepened on Clarissa's cheeks. She let out another sigh, and leaned her elbows on the table next to where Jane had begun clipping stems and coaxing them into place in the vase.

"I suppose I did complain a great deal back then about being stuck in a place with only female company. And, yes, I probably will be awful when I do lose my beauty and the gentlemen do stop courting me—oh, Jane, that is exactly why it is so important that I find someone who really loves me before then!"

Jane stopped cutting flower stems and paused to look at her friend. Ever since they had first met at school five years ago and Clarissa had bounced into the dining room, full of sunshine and smiles and plans, Jane had worshiped her friend. She had never seen anyone—or anything—as beautiful as Clarissa. And Clarissa had a way of making life seem magical and exciting.

But as of late a worm of envy had crept into her devotion. She still adored Clarissa, but she could not help but wish that just once, a gentleman might look at her—at Jane Preston, with her freckles and her maypole figure—and perhaps think her something special.

And Jane knew full well that this traitorous wish had begun when Sir Anthony Lee had stepped into Clarissa's court.

Clarissa barely noticed Sir Anthony. He wasn't a rake, and she scorned him for being the eldest of her suitors. But he was only thirty-four, which was not that old. He did not stand out by his dress, nor by his manners, nor by his looks. He had brown hair and eyes, and he was a little heavy—rather like a large, soft bear. But he was so kind. And he had a lovely, soft voice, almost like a rumbling purr.

But when he spoke to Jane in that melting, deep voice, he talked of Clarissa—of her beauty, and her vivacity, and her talents. And Jane had started to hate that. She hated herself even more for being so jealous and disloyal.

"Clarissa, you shall always be beautiful and adored," Jane said, stabbing a daffodil into place. "So stop talking such nonsense."

Turning, she saw the shadows cloud Clarissa's eyes, and her ill will vanished. She did not know what it was like to be beautiful, and to fear losing that beauty. Nor did she know what it was like to have a beloved father die. But she could imagine. And she knew how fragile Clarissa's confidence could be. She had been the one who had held Clarissa in her arms as she sobbed out her heart after the letter came, telling of her father's death and saying that she must go home from school. She had seen Clarissa's world crash around her.

Jane had known then that Clarissa would be the one to whom things happened. Tragedy and triumph would be Clarissa's. And she had been content to simply share in them vicariously. For she had also learned that Clarissa felt both of those far too deeply, and that if buffeted too much by life, she could be destroyed. Which made Jane determined to see her friend happy and safe in a marriage where she would be loved.

So, she put her arms around Clarissa and led her to the settee in the conservatory. After all, there was just the slightest chance that, after Clarissa reformed her rake, Sir Anthony's eyes might turn elsewhere.

"What is it that you are really worried about?"

Jane asked, happy to hear herself sounding practical as ever, and more like a friend again.

Clarissa fiddled with the leaf of a palm as it brushed against her arm. There were times when Jane could be maddeningly placid, and ridiculously shy. And yet she relied upon the strength at Jane's core. She wished at times that she, too, had such a core. But she knew also it was far more likely that she was the same as her mother—flighty and not really able to cope terribly well.

"You know exactly what I am worried about," she said. "It was bad enough with just Wolviston, but now I have St. Albans sending me flowers and writing me notes, and even Lady Havers is a little nervous that I have attracted two rakes. That's why she is having this dinner—so I can be seen in white, all demure and innocent, and so people will stop speculating about whether I am doing things that I should not be doing. And I only wish I were doing something that might actually justify the gossip, and make it clear if Wolviston really cares about—"

Clarissa broke off her speech. It sounded as tangled as her thoughts. She peered at Jane. "Are you certain you are not the least interested in Lord St. Albans?"

Face blanching, Jane shook her head, her reddish curls shaking lose and starting to tumble down. She pushed them back into place, muttering as she did, "I beg you, do not even think of him for me. He . . . oh, I cannot explain it. Wolviston merely intimidates me, while Lord St. Albans . . ."

"I know," Clarissa said, her mood glum. "He makes you squirm and wish almost to be back in the schoolroom, or at the least, very, very safely chaperoned. I do not quite understand it myself. With Lord Wolviston—oh, Jane, he really is deliciously dangerous. When he carried me to the carriage from the Opera House . . ."

She broke off with a sigh, unable to put into words the tingle that danced across her skin even now at the memory of Wolviston's arms around her, so strong and intensely male.

Jane let out her own deep sigh. "I know. You feel all warm and soft inside, as if there were a fire starting in the deepest part of you."

Sitting up, Clarissa stared at her friend. "How do you . . . ?"

"At least, that is what I imagine it is like," Jane added, her tone brisk. "But if you really do prefer Wolviston, what are you going to do with St. Albans?"

Getting up, Clarissa strode back to fuss with the flowers, plucking leaves off the roses that St. Albans had sent her. "Honestly, Jane, you make it sound as if he is a dress I ought to send back because he does not fit. I cannot do that. Besides, I am not at all certain yet that I want to marry either St. Albans or Wolviston."

"Well, I cannot blame you for having second thoughts. Rakes do seem to be rather uncomfortable sorts of men."

Clarissa frowned, and kept her other doubts to herself. The nagging suspicion had only recently come to her that perhaps Wolviston was not as much a rake as she had heard. It was the comparison between St. Albans—his sly innuendoes, his schemes to have her meet him in secret, his bold stares—and Wolviston which had started her doubts. Indeed,

Wolviston had twice rescued her from St. Albans's attention. Was that because of his own interest in her? Or from more admirable reasons? But, why had he not even tried to kiss her? Did he not desire her?

She had to learn the truth, and she had to do so before gossip made her into a compromised miss.

She turned around, her decision made. It would be a daring move, but she was in search of a daring man, after all. "I am very much afraid that I must resort to more direct tactics, Jane. I think I will need to kiss them both to decide."

Jane sat still, her mouth fallen open. Then alarm crept into her eyes. "Both? Does that not seem rather greedy?"

"Well, yes, it does. And, truth be told, I am not at all quite certain I really want to kiss Lord St. Albans—but if I do not I should not have any comparison for Lord Wolviston, now would I? And I do feel as if I owe them at least a fair comparison."

"But if anyone learns—oh, everyone will know for certain that you are fast. To kiss even one man and not marry him is beyond acceptable!"

"Why? It is not as if I have not had boys trying to kiss me in the back orchard since I was sixteen."

Jane frowned. "I do not think the world will see that as being anything like encouraging two rakes to take advantage of you."

"Nonsense. If no one finds out, then I am not ruined, am I? And how else am I to decide if there are any true and deep feelings between me and either man?"

Jane's frown deepened so that lines creased her forehead. "That may be, but how will you do it?"

Drawing in a breath, Clarissa wished she felt as

bold as her words. She knew just how much she risked. If things went wrong, she might well set herself beyond any hope of marriage. But if all went right . . .

"Tomorrow night. I am certain they will come, even though her ladyship has not invited them, but when has that ever stopped a rake? And I will need your help as I never have before, for I have to make certain that a kiss is all either man gets from me."

"You look ravishing," Lady Havers said, coming forward to greet Clarissa in the drawing room. Hands stretched out, wreathed in rose scent and rustling in a rich burgundy satin gown, she beamed at her goddaughter.

Clarissa's smile faltered. Her ladyship had chosen an unfortunate description. Would she be ravished tonight?

Despite the fires lit in the house, her fingers were cold, and nerves fluttered in her stomach worse than the night she had been presented to the aging Queen at court. But she would not back down. She had committed herself to action.

However, she wished desperately that her Aunt Maeve was with her tonight. For that she would even have put up with her Uncle Andrew's scowling, dark presence. But a letter had arrived only this morning with word that the expected baby still had not put in an appearance. Aunt Maeve was now confined to her bed, and fretting in her letters about her enforced inactivity. Clarissa had written back a brief letter, but had not wanted to burden her aunt with troubles, and so had edited herself heavily. Besides, how did one ask in a letter about the wisdom of kissing a rake?

She smiled now as Lady Havers inspected her, making her twirl around so that her gown would sparkle in the candlelight.

"I knew the silver would work. With your gold hair, it was a risky choice, but that hint of ice blue in the silk is just what was needed to carry it off to perfection. And the silver gauze overskirt makes you look an utter angel."

"Thank you," Clarissa said, her smile even more forced. She felt wretchedly un-angelic.

Taking her hands back, she fumbled with her long, white kid gloves. She had not wanted to worry her godmother any more than she wanted to cause her aunt any concern. However, she had run out of options. She needed the counsel of an older woman, and Lady Havers had married a rake for love herself.

So, striving for a casual tone, she asked, "How did you know, exactly, when you met Lord Havers that he was the right gentleman for you?"

Lady Havers took her arm to lead her to the couch before the fire. "Oh, I didn't. I disliked him a great deal at first. But love can be rather like a spring shower. One moment, the day seems clear and sunny, and then clouds creep up and suddenly it is raining. It was like that for me. I did not even know I was in love until my dear Lord Havers set my head spinning with his kisses."

Clarissa brightened. "He kissed you before you were married?"

"He would have done even more had not my father walked in. There was the most awful row then, with me crying, and Havers saying he would not marry me. But that was before my father took him aside and told him it was marriage and ten thousand pounds, or prosecution for damaging his property—meaning me, of course. It was quite lowering to be talked of as if I were no more than a dairy cow who had been led astray from her pasture."

"But I thought you married for love," Clarissa said, confused.

Lady Havers blinked and smiled. "I did. But my lord certainly did not. It was not until months later that he actually said that he loved me. But, then, gentlemen are often so much more confused about their feelings than we are. It comes from that rational sense of theirs always getting in the way of what they feel. Ah, listen . . . I do believe I hear the first carriage arriving. How I do love to hold these little soirées. You must remind me to do this more often."

With a swish of skirts, Lady Havers rose and moved away to instruct her servants on dealing with the arriving guests.

Clarissa stayed seated, her fingers icy and her head spinning. What if she did fall in love—and he did not? She did not want that. No, it all seemed wrong, and not at all what she had in mind. She had been certain that the right man would love her, and then she would know that he was perfect because he did love her. And she had no father to insist that a marriage would take place. In fact, her uncle was far more likely to shoot any man whom he thought might have compromised her. Or to simply bundle her back to Yorkshire for the rest of her days.

She worried the fingertip of her glove, tugging it loose and then smoothing it back in place.

Lady Havers must have got it wrong. In Mr. Richardson's novel, *Clarissa,* did not the rakish Lovelace fall in love with the virtuous Clarissa? Did he not break his heart for her? And in real life, had not every one of her other suitors tried to offer up their hearts to her? Men always declared themselves to the woman they adored. Of course they did. It must be so.

But the thought lingered that perhaps it would be a good thing if neither Wolviston nor St. Albans came tonight to put her theories to the test.

Two hours later, Clarissa scanned the crowded drawing room. She had managed to send away her various admirers, one to fetch her a drink, another to procure her a plate of food, and four others to go with him and make selections that might tempt her. For the first time that evening, she did not have to smile and look amused and be charming.

She let out a breath of air, and stole away to a curtained alcove where she might observe the company without being accosted by yet another admirer.

Neither Wolviston nor St. Albans had arrived. Relief that they had not come now mixed with irritation that they had found other attractions.

Of course, Lady Havers had been delighted to see her surrounded by nothing but respectable young gentlemen. However, a dozen respectable gentlemen made a poor substitute for one particular wayward one.

Then a deep voice intruded into the alcove, sending shivers up Clarissa's spine. "Ah, Miss Derhurst, you look a fairy queen tonight—and one about to cast a rather dangerous spell on someone."

Eight

Turning, Clarissa found Lord St. Albans before her, sinfully sleek in his black evening clothes. The candlelight drew gold glints from his artfully curled hair, and an unsettling gleam danced in his green eyes, like flashes of something half-seen in deep water.

She fell back a step and he came into the alcove, letting the curtain fall closed behind him. The thick velvet muffled the noise and chatter from the formal drawing room, so that the space became at once too warm, too small, too isolated.

Clarissa fumbled for her fan and her poise. "Lord St. Albans, what a pleasure to see you."

"Is it?" he said, his tone dry and teasing. "You don't sound very pleased."

She snapped open her fan and turned away from him, pulling aside the curtain to view the other room and to remind herself that she was not really alone with him. She did not trust that too-eager look in his eyes. "Very well then, I am not pleased."

His low chuckle drew her gaze back to him. He was all contrasts and contradictions. Sharp edges and smooth manners. Repelling and attracting. His black coat and pantaloons fitted smooth over thoroughbred muscles, although he moved as if he were the laziest lord in London. His shirt and waistcoat gleamed white, as spotless as his reputation was not. From the folds of his cravat, a ruby winked like a drop of heart's blood.

But it was the hot glitter in his eyes that had her fidgeting with her fan. The fierce aroma of brandy set her nose twitching and put her other senses on alert. He had been drinking. Quite a lot, she suspected. Of course, she knew that rakes drank, but she was not well-pleased with him that he had come to her in this condition. It certainly did not bode well as a sign that he might reform his ways.

He stepped closer. "Do you know, I think I prefer you when you are not pleased. Anger adds a captivating flaw to your perfection."

She frowned at him, annoyed by his criticism. Yes, flattery bored her. But she hardly wanted a listing of her faults.

Lifting her chin, she eyed him, striving for a suitable chill in her gaze. "Does it? Then shall I give you such a demonstration of it that it utterly enthralls you?"

He gave a laugh. "Such sharp claws tonight, my sweet mystery. Shall I see, instead, if I can smooth your ruffled fur?" He came another step closer, and she stepped back. The velvet curtain brushed her arm, reminding her that it screened them from the room.

St. Albans loomed over her, his body so near that the heat from him seemed almost suffocating. Brandy fumes wound around her like a magical haze. His eyelids drooped low over those gleaming green eyes and her pulse began to hammer in her throat with a sickening force.

Voice soft, he asked, "Shall I show you how well I know how to sweeten a lady's temper?"

He swept her up against him, his grip hard and harsh. His brandy-soaked breath washed over her. Her stomach lurched. She pushed hard against him but he held her fast. Anger fired hot inside her like a burst of fireworks.

Suddenly, she hated his touch on her. This wasn't what she had pictured. She wanted sweet coaxing. A romantic moment. A tender scene. A touching of her soul, not just her body. Raw panic skittered loose inside her as his face loomed over hers.

No, not this way, her mind cried out. And her body reacted.

Clutching her fan hard, she snapped the ivory sticks and then shoved the broken fan toward his face with one hand while pushing on his chest with the other. He had to lean away from the broken ivory sticks and loosen his hold.

She slipped past him then, so that he no longer stood between her and the safety of the crowded room.

For an instant, she stood there, her mind blank as her thoughts struggled to catch up with what she had done. What was wrong with her? Why had she not let him kiss her? But even the thought of it could still stir a sour taste in her mouth and shiver fear along her skin like a drop of cold water.

How mortifying to find that one cannot even properly be improper, she thought, a little ill at her own bad manners in wishing for something only to cast it aside.

But what should she tell him now?

She glanced down at her broken fan, then looked up and stammered, "My fan. Pray, excuse me, Lord St. Albans. My father gave it to me before he died, and I must see if it can be repaired."

Before he could say anything, she turned and hurried from the alcove. Her cheeks warmed as hushed whispers followed her abrupt exit and her flustered path across the room. She glanced back only once.

St. Albans had stepped forward from the alcove, one white hand holding back the velvet curtain. His mouth twisted with impatience, but otherwise his face assumed an implacable mask that frightened her even more than had that gleam in his eyes. She could not imagine him as a man who bore with frustration well. And then her own anger flared as she thought of how really awful it had been of him to act as if she were . . . well, as if she were one of his brazen creatures.

Without another glance back, she stopped beside her aunt to show her broken fan. Her hasty explanation sounded babbling and confused to her, but Lady Havers only looked concerned and patted her hand when Clarissa said that she would be but a moment to repair her fan.

Then Clarissa fled the room and its tittering whispers. She knew that others were speculating about why she was leaving, but Lady Havers would tell them all that it was only a fuss over a broken fan. And perhaps no one would really notice Lord St. Albans's vexed expression.

Clutching her fan, she paused only to pick up a candlestick and take it with her.

In the conservatory, Jakes, the gardener, kept wire

to brace flower stems and glue to repair broken vases. But they—and her fan—were excuses, really. Once inside the dim room, she set down the candle and broken fan. Then she tugged off her gloves and pressed cold palms to her hot cheeks.

Oh, she had just told the most awful set of lies to make good on her escape.

The fan was not the one her father had given her on her thirteenth birthday. That one—also of ivory, but made of white silk and spangles—lay safely up in its sandalwood box in her room. This one was a mere trifle that she had bought not two weeks ago at Harding, Howell and Company's.

She let out a small sigh. She really must make certain that St. Albans did not learn about her little deception, for she had the feeling that scowl of his would darken even more. And a cold tremor ran across her skin when she wondered how he might plan to take his revenge against her.

"What did he do to you?"

Spinning around, she braced her hands on the table behind her.

Lord Wolviston stood before her, half hidden in shadows. Like St. Albans, he too wore black. In the golden light, the silver threads in his brocade waistcoat glinted like pricks of starlight. She could not see his expression, only that his gray eyes seemed as gloomy as a Yorkshire winter's day.

Well, she was quite fed up with rakes and their poor manners and unpredictable actions. So she snapped, "Why must you rakes sneak about like that? Can you not simply walk into a room? And he did nothing to me."

She looked away, half afraid that if she did not

bark at him like this, she might give in to the urge
to throw herself into his arms and beg him to look
after her as he had at the masquerade. But that was
silly. He had not said that he wanted to look after
anyone but himself. And she could, after all, look
after herself quite well.

But once she looked away she had to look back
again. Would he leave her alone now? She desperately hoped not, for what if St. Albans had also followed her?

Wolviston's frown darkened, and then he stepped
into the small pool of golden candlelight. He glanced
down at the broken fan on the table and touched a
lean, sun-browned finger to one still-intact stick. He
wore no gloves, and Clarissa realized that she liked
that he hardly ever did so. He had lovely hands. Capable hands, which looked as if they knew work, unlike St. Albans's pale and too-elegant fingers.

She gave a small sigh, for Wolviston never put his
hands on her much, anyway. Not like St. Albans did.

"I walked into quite a buzz tonight about you having escaped an encounter with St. Albans. Is this all
he damaged?"

With a small shrug, she waved away the gossip.
"He did nothing. Nothing at all! I did it myself."

Reaching up, he touched her arm, barely brushing his fingertips across her bare skin. "Then why
are you trembling?"

Her stare slid away from his to focus on the ivory
sticks and the discarded flowers that lay strewn
across the table. She did not want to admit that St.
Albans had nearly kissed her. Somehow, what she
had almost done did not seem romantic or daring.
It only seemed horrid, like a bad dream. And she

certainly did not want him to know how shaken it had left her. He would think her a very silly girl, then, without any experience of the world.

"Nothing happened. Nothing ever happens," she said, her voice small and tight and miserable, despite the fact that she wanted it to be sultry, sophisticated, and seasoned.

His tone turned dry. "With you involved, I find that difficult to believe."

He stood still for a moment, and when she did not answer, he moved away. She thought he would go, and she pressed her lips tightly together, thinking how vastly aggravating men were, and how she wished she had a good solid vase within reach so she could fling it at his heartless back. But when she looked up, she saw that he was only moving away to gather the wire and glue that she had come here with the excuse of seeking.

With an effort, he stripped off his black evening coat and flung it onto a wrought iron settee. In his shirtsleeves, he set to work.

She stood beside the table, her lower lip caught between her teeth as he bent over her fan. The candle cast a warm glow onto his skin, and turned his hair into a luscious blend of warm browns, like the finest polished rosewood.

Scraping the toe of one satin slipper against the flagstone floor, she watched him, guilt stealing into her. "You need not bother with it, really."

He glanced at her. "Lady Havers said you had it from your father."

She looked away. Oh, why had she uttered that lie to her ladyship? But she had been too flustered to think of why else the fan should be so important to her, and now he was putting all this effort out for the merest nothing.

He turned back to the fan, and she shifted from one foot to the other until she had to see what he was doing. Edging closer, she leaned over his shoulder.

The soft lawn of his shirt brushed her arm. He did not seem to notice her, and so she leaned even closer, all too aware of the crisp smell of his shirt and of him.

A shadow of beard brushed his cheek, outlining the strong line of his chin. He had a small freckle near his right ear. And a curl of brown hair lay just in front of it. Her fingers itched to smooth that wayward curl. But he probably would not like that, so she tried to focus on her worthless fan, not on him.

Gentle but efficient, he straightened each stick, matching the breaks and smoothing the silk as if it were a living thing. Twice he turned the fan over, cradling it between his own large hands, so that the mended bits would not fall apart. His touch fascinated her. What would it be like to be so gently soothed, so carefully stroked, so expertly handled?

At last, he straightened.

Clarissa stared down at her fan. The empty conservatory seemed oddly warm, and she did not know what to do with her hands, except to tug at the fingers of one hand with the others. Why did it seem so different to stand here, so close to Wolviston? Why did he not cause the panic in her that St. Albans had? What was it about him that made her want him to take her in his arms?

Her fan was by no means made perfect, but it was whole again. And he had gone to all this effort for something not worth five shillings. Her chin drooped and misery lay tight and cold in her.

He gave her a slow smile. "I wouldn't recommend using it to give any gentleman a playful rap on his knuckles, but you should be able to carry it without getting any odd looks."

She went over to the settee and picked up his coat. The fabric had wrinkled and she smoothed her hand over the cloth before bringing it to him.

Looking up at him, she tried to find something else to say to him. What should she say? Thank you, you need not have bothered? I could have bought another one?

"What's wrong?" he asked.

She shook her head, then said, "Nothing."

Looking away, he frowned, then he seemed to make up his mind about something, for he turned back to her, his expression set and his eyes darkening. "Clarissa, I came tonight, hoping to see you. Alone."

She looked up, a bubble of anticipation blooming like a hot house flower. "Yes. I mean, you did?"

"I . . . well, I wanted to tell you that I—that is, what you've heard—I mean, well, what I want to say is that you have been misled. I am not as bad as gossip has said."

She smiled at him. He wanted her to think good of him. Was that not the first step to reform, to wish for a better reputation? Was that why he had spent all this effort for her?

"How could I think ill of you when you went to all this bother for me?" she said.

His frown deepened, and he rubbed the back of

his neck. "That is not what I mean. It's not just the matter of a mended fan."

She stepped closer, his coat folded over her arm. "Then what do you mean?"

"I mean—the rumors about me, you should not believe them."

"Of course not. Rumors are so hateful. The ones starting up about me aren't true, either."

His head jerked up. "What rumors?"

She came a step closer. "Nothing, really. Just the gossip that an unmarried young lady must expect when she attracts the attention of two rakes. There are those who speculate that perhaps I am not as innocent as I ought to be."

Wolviston cursed under his breath and pinched the bridge of his nose. Damn, but he seemed to be leading her on a merry dance toward social ruin. Because he had wanted a bit of fun. And because she had bruised his pride.

Well, it would end. Here and now.

Straightening, he looked her in the eye. "Clarissa, I have to tell you that I am not what you think I am."

She came one step closer, so close that he could not tell her sweet scent apart from that of the hyacinths around them. So close he could see the soft rise and fall of her breasts, half bared by her gown. So close that he could easily reach out to touch the golden curl that danced next to that slim, white neck of hers.

"But I know who you are," she said, her voice breathy and low.

She smiled at him, and his senses reeled. The air went out his chest. As a boy, he had been kicked square in the chest by a foal. That was nothing compared to how her glowing smile, her curving lips, and her shining eyes knocked into him now. His mouth dried so that he could only shake his head that she did not know him at all.

But she went on, heedless of his unvoiced denial. "You are a man who needs someone to say, 'I do not care what is in your past, so long as I can share your present.' You are someone who has for too long been alone. Even when you are in a room of people, you are not with them. You are a man who needs refuge, not from the world, but from yourself."

Her voice flowed over him like a spring brook over a desert, sinking into crevices he had not known existed, starting to sprout desires that had lain dormant inside him.

He tried to laugh and tell her that he did not want any such thing. What nonsense. He wanted a bit of fun. He wanted a fine lark—and he was having one, damn it. He wanted nothing more.

And, yet . . . and yet . . .

How nice, a small voice in him whispered . . . how lovely it would be to hear her say this to him and to have her mean it. *I do not care what your past is—I only want to share your present.*

But she would care.

She'd do more than care, once she found out he was a fantasy built exclusively for her. Oh, she would care that he had played her for a fool, right enough.

Or he could become that rake for her. Right now. By kissing her senseless.

Only, damn it, that wasn't supposed to be how this went. She was the one who was supposed to learn a lesson about judging a man before she met him. He wasn't the one here to learn how to be a rogue and a devil.

This had all gone wrong. She was not even listening to his explanations that he wasn't what she thought he was. He ought to leave. Now. Before he gave in to those impulses stirring inside him. It was spending all that time in those damn brothels that had fired his blood and left him vulnerable to her charms. Once he was outside in the cool spring air, good sense would return and these mad desires would leave.

He cleared his throat and said, his voice a rough growl in his own ears, "I must go."

He stretched out his hand for his jacket, and his fingers closed over hers. And then he began pulling his coat from her, and somehow she came along with it until she stood before him, so close that now all he had to do was bend down to kiss her.

"Thank you for putting my fan right," she said, staring up at him, her eyes as endlessly deep as enchanted pools. They had the faintest flecks of green in them. She gave his coat over to him, and then her hands spread open on his chest, slipping under the edges of his brocade waistcoat. "Can you put me to rights as well?"

His head bent closer to hers. He could not stop its movement and he did not want to. Without any effort she drew him closer, just with that soft firing of desire in her eyes.

"There's nothing to repair in you," he said.

She nodded. "But there . . ."

His lips took the rest of her words, swallowing them in the quick gasp of surprise she released when his mouth touched hers. His tongue brushed across those lips, seeking only a taste, but finding far more. And then he forgot why he should not kiss her. Why he should not hold her. Why he was not really a rake.

His coat rustled to the floor, and her hands found their own path to steal around his neck and pull him closer. His fingers roved up her bare arms and tangled in her hair, and her mouth opened, shy and yet as eager as his own.

Desire poured into him from where her lips met his, filling him with reckless abandon, and then, his breathing ragged, his blood raging, he managed to drag his head away from her.

Damn it. Here she was again, leading him away from his purpose. And he was not going to have it.

Easing her hands from their grasp around his neck, he pushed her away.

She stared up at him. Her eyes shone as if that embrace had put fairy dust in them. Her lips, red and swollen, begged for more kisses.

Stooping, he bent to retrieve his coat, glad of the excuse to turn away. Dear God, he needed to turn away before he did something they would both regret. He did not want a wife, and she did not want a country gentleman for a husband, and he would do well to remember that before they *had* to marry and spend the rest of their lives hating each other for it.

Puzzled, Clarissa watched as Wolviston took up his coat, brushed at it, and then shrugged into it, as casual as if he kissed a lady every day. Which he probably did, she realized, with a raw stab of jealousy twisting her stomach. She waited for him to say something—anything that indicated what he felt.

That kiss had done more than set her head spinning. It had burned from her lips to her toes, and then sizzled back up and into her core, branding her in ways she could not explain. Her mouth still tingled. And she ached for more.

Yet, he stood there, brushing a bit of dust from his sleeve, seeming not to care.

"Well?" she asked, impatient with his silence.

"Well, what?" Wolviston said, his tone so blunt that he winced at the sound of it in his own ears.

He tried not to look at her. He disliked how his words had dimmed the light in her eyes, and he disliked himself even more for living up to his manufactured reputation. He tried to work up a justified anger. She had, after all, no right to go around allowing men such as himself access to those perfect lips. But he had been the one to kiss her—and, Lord help him, he wanted to do so again.

With his coat on, he faced her, wishing that the black broadcloth provided some sort of armor against that pouting beauty. What devil had ever put that combination of reckless innocence and loveliness together? She lowered her chin and stared up at him, seeming more girl than woman and stirring an urge in him to pull her into a comforting embrace.

Only it wouldn't stay that way. He would not stop at offering comfort, not when he had that luscious body in his arms again.

And so he took her chin between his thumb and forefinger, tilted her head up, and scowled at her, playing his role for all it was worth. If she wanted a rake, he would give her one now. Perhaps this performance might wean her of romantic notions.

"Consider that, my beauty, fair payment for the repairs. And, next time, take more care, or you may find that more than your fan gets broken."

He had the heart-twisting satisfaction of seeing her eyes darken with wounded confusion and then spark with outrage. Striding past her, he half expected a potted plant, or a vase at the least, to sail past his ear. He deserved it.

But he heard no more than a small, sharp sigh, as if something else other than a fan had indeed broken behind him.

"You did what?" Reggie said, his voice rising so much that even the rowdiest patrons of The Rose tavern in Russell Street paused to glance over to Wolviston's table. It was a wet night outside, and a slow one inside.

Lifting his brandy glass, Wolviston shot a quelling glance around at the curious stares, and then turned back to his friend. "Why don't you just stand on the table and shout out that I kissed the Derhurst girl, so that I'll have to marry her for certain?"

Reggie blushed to the roots of his ginger hair. "Sorry. But from the sound of it, you hardly need my shouting. You're going to have to marry her, you know."

Wolviston scowled. The same thought had nagged at him for the past two days, ever since he had fled Lady Havers's conservatory and her house. Too much conditioning to act the gentleman, he knew. A gentleman, after all, did not kiss a lady unless he meant to marry her—or unless she was no lady.

"I know nothing of the sort," he insisted, hoping

that if he told himself so enough times he would start to believe it. "I did not compromise her."

"Yet. And that kiss must have given her some expectations that you will marry her."

"Oh, give over, man. She wanted to be kissed by a rake. . . ."

"And she wants to marry a rake."

"So I kissed her. That's all."

"And she hopes to reform a rake," Reggie said, and then he jabbed the air with his tankard of ale to emphasize the point.

"Well, she can't reform me if I simply bow out of her lists."

Reggie sat up, his plump chin mulishly jutting forward. "You may bow out, but where will that leave her, I ask you?"

Wolviston drank back his brandy and then lifted his hand for the tavern wench and a third round. "It will leave her, I hope, more apt to look for a respectable fellow."

Reggie snorted, and then waited as a buxom lass sauntered over with fresh drinks. She offered Wolviston a bold stare and a wink. He tossed two half crowns onto her wooden tray. A moment later she seemed to realize that would be all she got from him and she left with a pouting frown.

Starting to nurse the next brandy, Wolviston stared at Reggie and hoped like the devil that the fellow would leave the subject alone. Clarissa had become a sore topic with him.

He was not, he told himself, in love with that willful, conceited little beauty. No, he was not one of those calf-eyed idiots who crowded around her, begging for crumbs of her attention. No and no and no!

"Have you thought about telling her the truth?" Reggie demanded, interrupting Wolviston's argument between his thoughts and his feelings.

Wolviston gave a harsh laugh. "The truth, old son, could dazzle in her eyes with the glow of a million candles and she would say it is still dark. Yes, I've tried. She seemed to think I was confessing my true, inner good nature."

Reggie frowned. "You must not have tried hard enough."

His glass paused in midair, Wolviston glared at his friend. Then he drank back the sharp amber liquid and let it burn down his throat. The devil of it was that Reggie was right. He had not tried very hard. And he certainly did not want to try again.

God help him, it had been bad enough to see her eyes darken with hurt when he had brushed off that kiss as being of no matter. His throat tightened and his stomach knotted when he thought of how she might react to his full confession that he had played a May-game with her. Her anger he could take, but he came undone now at the thought that she might dissolve in tears before him. If that happened, he might start saying things that would have him end up leg-shackled to her.

And he did not want a wife. He had worn the responsibility of a family—of his brothers and his mother and even his father—for his entire youth. He wanted some time for himself. He wanted to enjoy this adventure, damn it.

Glumly, Reggie stared first into his half-empty tankard and then blearily looked up at Wolviston.

"Well, if you're going to drop her, that means it'll fall to me to keep her—and Jane—out of St. Albans's path."

"What do you mean, up to you?"

"Someone must. Fellow's a rogue. And so are you. St. Albans ain't going to bow out of the list. He ain't going to stop."

Wolviston opened his mouth to protest, but a third male voice answered for him. "Speak of the devil . . . and here I am. But just what am I not going to stop?"

Nine

Wolviston glanced up and into St. Albans's face and he thought how very much he would enjoy blackening the man's eyes. However, he had no real excuse to pick a fight. And the weight of Clarissa's good name, already linked too closely with him and St. Albans, lay heavy as a hand on his shoulder.

Biting back his dislike, he gestured to an empty wooden chair. The Rose was not noted for its fine furnishings. Decades of smoke stained its paneled walls, and the tables and chairs all bore the scars from knife fights, broken glasses, and hard wear. So did many of its patrons.

St. Albans pulled the chair to Wolviston's corner table, took out a lawn handkerchief, dusted the seat, and made himself comfortable. After pulling off his gloves, he gestured for service, ordered a brandy from the sloe-eyed tavern wench, and then turned back to Wolviston.

"Now what is it that I am not going to stop? I do enjoy hearing the stories put out about me." He spoke in a drawling tone, but Wolviston caught the edge of steel in his voice and the hard glint in his eyes. So he had upset St. Albans, had he? The evening looked to improve. He might not be able to start a decent brawl, but he would enjoy making the fellow uncomfortable.

Wolviston lounged back in his chair. "Reggie was just offering a bet that nothing would stop you from going to hell in a hand-basket. I do wonder why it must always be in a hand-basket? Perhaps for the convenience of it?"

His eyes narrowing, St. Albans glanced at Reggie's suddenly pale face. "You offered a bet about me?"

"No. I mean, yes. I mean . . . well, Evan can explain better that I, can't you, Evan, old son?" Reggie said, glaring at his friend with a look that promised retribution for being put on the spot.

St. Albans turned back to Wolviston. "Can you really?"

Wolviston grinned. "What's wrong, St. Albans? Don't you like sport being made of your good name? Oh, I forgot. You don't have a good name, do you?"

For an instant, the pulse beat faster in St. Albans's jaw. Wolviston sat still, his muscles tensed for action.

Then St. Albans relaxed back into his chair. "I do my best not to. As do you, sir. But if you must have some sport tonight, what say we make a small wager, eh? I shall stake you a hundred to one that I can bed twice the number of women you can before tomorrow's sun rises? Are you up for that bet?"

Reggie choked on his drink, but Wolviston merely cocked an eyebrow. "Sorry. Not interested. I have always preferred quality to quantity."

St. Albans's drink arrived. He paid the wench with a silver shilling that had her eyes widening at such generosity; then he turned back to Wolviston. "Quality is it? How odd it is, then, that at every quality establishment I know of in London, you, sir, are not known. Now, why could that be?"

Wolviston met St. Albans's knowing smirk. Obviously, St. Albans suspected something was amiss with Wolviston's rakish reputation. However, if he actually knew anything, he would not be here, fishing for information. So, Wolviston merely smiled back and said, "What a flattering interest you show. I could, of course, tell you that my business is none of your affair. But I will tell you instead that the quality I seek is difficult to come by in a shop. And what challenge is there, after all, in buying a woman's pretense of affection?"

"A smooth answer, indeed." St. Albans raised his glass. "Let us drink to challenges then."

Wolviston drank the toast, while Reggie frowned and looked as if he would rather be anywhere but in The Rose and drinking with St. Albans. However, Wolviston had had his curiosity stirred. He disliked that the fellow had been nosing around. But what had roused St. Albans's suspicions? And what would put them to rest?

Pulling out a silver snuffbox inlaid with mother-of-pearl in the shape of Venus rising from the sea, St. Albans flipped it open with his thumb and offered the moist tobacco around. Reggie and Wolviston both declined, and St. Albans said, as he took a pinch, "What virtue you gentlemen show. It is a good thing the ladies are not here to see what Puritans you can be. It so disappoints them when they find that we are not such wicked souls as they would like us to be."

Wolviston's smile tightened at St. Albans's veiled threat. Now he understood the man's game. He could just see St. Albans, all eager solace, offering Clarissa a shoulder to cry upon after filling her ears with stories about the pretend rake who had tricked her. Well, he'd see this devil in hell before that happened.

With a sharp rap, he set his glass down upon the scarred oak table. "If you still want a wager, St. Albans, what say we go gaming? I know a snug hell not far from here. Are you up for that sport?"

St. Albans's golden brows lifted over his glittering green eyes. "Am I? Well, well, it might be interesting to see what the night brings." He drank back his brandy, rose, and then started for the door.

Wolviston also rose to his feet, but Reggie leaned across the table, caught his wrist, and said, his voice low and urgent, "Are you mad or drunk?"

He shook off Reggie's grip and leaned his palms on the table, offering up a reckless grin. "Does it matter which? Come on, old son. The evening is young and we've drunk a toast to challenges. I have a devil's reputation to cement tonight. And if St. Albans is with me, then at least I know he's not luring Clarissa into trouble."

"Perhaps I should become a nun," Clarissa said, leaning closer to Jane so that others would not hear.

Jane gave her back a frown and whispered behind her fan, "Don't be such a goose—you are not even Catholic."

They sat at the edge of Almack's main room, which had been hired for a private party to which Lady Havers had been invited. The first assembly of the season would actually be held the week after Easter Sunday, and Clarissa had been looking forward to an early glimpse of Society's fabled Marriage Mart—the place where Dukes and Earls came to choose their brides.

It utterly disappointed most of her fantasies.

Of course she found it a pretty enough set of rooms, with high ceilings and elegant proportions. The musicians sat in a raise box at one end, crystal hung from double-tiered chandeliers, and scarves draped the long windows. Chairs had been set along the wall so that those not dancing could admire those who were.

But Clarissa found she did not care for that view at all.

Because Almack's had not officially opened and she had not yet been given permission to waltz, she had had to decline any offers to dance this set. Lady Havers insisted on being overly conservative on this point. So Clarissa sat with Jane, smiling and watching other ladies who smugly twirled and stepped past with such a superior air that she almost wished she had stayed home.

Lady Havers's elation over the invitation sent by Lady Cowper had made Clarissa think this evening must rank as one of the ultimate treats of the season. Her ladyship had hinted that they might meet the famous poet, Lord Byron, or perhaps even the exquisite Mr. Brummell, who had led fashion for so many years.

But Clarissa found no such interesting company in attendance.

And, actually, there was just one gentleman she had really hoped to see here tonight, for she had not seen him anywhere else for the past two days.

However, the only gentlemen here seemed to be mincing ones who craned their necks to check the mirror for their own reflection, and gray-haired men who looked old enough to be her grandfather.

As for the ladies, well, she noted painfully shy girls, terribly snobbish girls, and ladies far too old for the low-cut dresses they wore. If they were Society's elite, perhaps Society was not as wonderful as it thought itself.

Clarissa gave a sigh and began to pleat the ribbon on the front of her white silk gown. "I do not mean a real nun, Jane. I meant that perhaps I should just say that I am going to take my vows. Do you think it might alarm him, that I might become unobtainable?"

"It would certainly alarm your family. Do you want them descending on you?"

"Oh, they would not. I had another letter from home and Aunt Maeve is still increasing. Mother wrote that Uncle Andrew said he had seen peasant women in Spain who did not grow as huge, and that she looks as if she is carrying a litter."

Jane giggled, and then to hide such a vulgar display of emotion in these stuffy rooms, she covered her mouth with a hand encased in elbow-length kidskin. "Oh, dear. Your mother cannot have approved of that quip."

"She did not. She also swears she will take to her bed any day now. I think she is suffering from sympathy pains—or perhaps she simply does not like that Aunt Maeve is getting all the attention of late."

"Clarissa! You should not speak so about your mother."

"But it is true. And you know it is."

"That does not mean you should say it. And I do not think this plan to announce your nunship will do anything. Besides, it has only been two days since you last saw Lord Wolviston. You should concentrate on being an appropriately simpering miss, just like the rest of us here."

"You are not simpering, Jane. And if you become so, I shall disown you. And it is all very well for you to say it has been only two days, but it feels as if it has been forever."

Frowning, Clarissa thought she could not go on like this for much longer, both hoping to see him and hoping not to. After that kiss, she had spent the rest of the evening smiling, talking, and aching inside. She had gone to bed and tossed and turned, beating a pillow that would not be comfortable and inventing clever things that she should have said to him.

She ought to have told him that she had had better kisses—only that was such a lie. She ought to have said that he had labored over a fan that meant even less to her than he did. Only that was a lie as well. And she ought to have told him that she would break fans—and hearts—as she pleased. That, at least, was not a lie.

Only it seemed far too close to the truth that she might be in danger of breaking her own heart.

But she was not in love with him. No, she could not be. If she had been, her heart would be light, not leaden. But that kiss had changed her. It had shaken her, right down to her toes, and she still felt as if he had left her in pieces that she did not know how to put together again.

What should she say to him when next they met?

Should she look for opportunities to place her practiced barbs? Or should she act as if she could not even remember his kiss?

And then an even more terrible thought wrapped around her heart and tightened.

"Jane, what if he does not want to see me again—ever?"

Jane took Clarissa's gloved hand in her own. "Stop that. Reggie told me he was seeing Lord Wolviston tonight, so he has not left London, which means that you must see him sometime."

"Well, obviously I do not seem to figure in his plans, that is for certain," Clarissa said, tracing the gold embroidery that decorated the overskirt to her gown.

"What is this, the sulks?" Jane asked, her voice sharp. "I vow I do not know this mouse who sits here, her heart on her sleeve, when any idiot can see that of course Lord Wolviston must try to keep his distance. He is fighting his attraction to you."

Scowling, Clarissa glanced up. "If he is, he is doing a rather too good job at it."

"If he did not care for you, he would have done more than kiss you in the conservatory—and then he would have left you there, ruined and alone. The fact that he tried to be awful to you after he kissed you, so that you might start to hate him, makes it obvious that he really is starting to feel something for you. He is trying to protect you from himself."

Clarissa bit her lower lip and looked away, staring at a sweet-faced, fair-haired woman who sat by herself, looking rather expectant and uncertain. *And that is just how I feel,* Clarissa thought, *expecting everything and certain of nothing.*

However, Jane had a point. If it had been St. Albans with her in that empty conservatory, she doubted that he would have stopped at taking a kiss.

"If that is the case, then how can I make him stop protecting me? The problem is that we ladies are not supposed to do anything but wait and I am not very good at waiting, so I must do something."

"Just do not do something foolish," Jane said.

Clarissa could not resist an impish smile. "You mean I should not arrange for him to save me from danger?"

Jane scowled, and Clarissa gave a laugh. "You are too easy to tease. No, I am not about to do that. It seems I cannot even lure him into paying a morning call on me, let alone ride to my rescue. But it would be nice if I could stage an act of daring, for he does seem to enjoy being gallant . . . in fact, Jane, has it ever occurred to you that, for a rake, Lord Wolviston is rather, well, he is rather a gentleman?"

"Of course he is. He is a viscount and a lord."

"It is not just that. There is a quality about him. A . . . a steadfastness. After all, here I am talking about luring him to me, but should he not, as a rake, be luring me to him? After all, I do not have to do the least luring of Lord St. Albans. He brought me a fan the other day to replace the one I broke to escape his kiss and has been nothing but charming. I quite like him when he is so charming. But somehow it is rather like having a charming tiger loose about one—one has the feeling that claws and sharp teeth are not that far away from one."

With a scowl, Jane said, "Not that charming a tiger."

"Well, he can be. And I do wish I could like him

better. He can be very droll, you know. But then he gets that look in his eyes and—well, I feel as if it does not matter to him, really, whether it is me or any other woman with him. In fact, there are times that I have wondered if he is interested in me only because I do not seem interested in him."

"And Wolviston?" Jane asked, a worried edge to her voice.

Clarissa let out a sigh. "I am not at all certain he really is interested in me either."

The musicians ended the waltz with a flourish, and the dancers bowed and curtsied. Clarissa and Jane both rose to look about for the gentlemen who might be next to dance with them, but then a hush fell over the room. Gentlemen and ladies turned toward the entrance, and a charge seemed to sweep in as if a storm were approaching.

Clarissa and Jane glanced at each other and then followed the other stares to the entrance.

A gentleman stood in the doorway, dressed in the formal knee breeches and evening clothes required by Almack's. He had on a dark blue coat and pale blue waistcoat, but Clarissa found her attention riveted by his face.

His skin stood out, pale as white marble and just as lustrous. Dark curls, which held glints of chestnut, emphasized his interesting pallor. He had an arrogant, cleft chin and an air about him as if he were dismissive of everyone present. Sharp and piercing, as if made of blue-steel, his eyes swept over the room, his stare seeming to search for one particular face.

Like wind through trees, shocked whispers swept

the room, and Clarissa heard a lady mutter, in a breathy, dreamy voice, "Byron."

Byron started across the room, his step halting with that slight limp which Clarissa had heard other ladies say made him so interesting. He made his way toward the woman who sat by herself and whom Clarissa had noticed earlier. She had been ignored by everyone—but not by Lord Byron.

As Byron approached, the woman's vague expression changed to a charming smile. She stood and reached out gloved hands to welcome him, and Clarissa wondered who she was that Byron would single her out for his attention.

Then Lady Havers hurried up to them, catching Clarissa and Jane with each of her hands, and starting them to the doors. "Come, girls. It is time to go. Hurry now."

"But are we not to meet Lord Byron?" Clarissa asked, trying to hold back. She glanced around. Others had started to leave, turning their backs on Byron and the sweet-faced, fair-haired lady he had sought out. The dowagers glanced at the couple and looked away—and Clarissa caught her breath. The cut direct. What had Byron and that poor woman done to deserve such scorn from these grand dames?

Lady Havers cast a dismayed glance at the man with piercing, arrogant eyes and the stubborn chin. She gave a sigh and then urged Clarissa and Jane to the red carpeted stairs again. "It is too bad to have invited them both. They really should have left poor Augusta out of this. I would wager that Sally Jersey, or perhaps Emily Cowper, dear soul that she is, thought all would be forgiven, but they really ought to have known better than to throw both of them together in public."

"What is to be forgiven?" Clarissa asked.

"Everything, my dear," Lady Havers said, heavy meaning in her voice. Then she led the girls down the stairs.

As they waited with others in the entry hall for their carriage to be brought around, the gossip swelled around them.

"Why, did you see how Augusta Leigh greeted him?"

"Yes, but she is his half-sister, after all."

"But Lady Byron left him because of her, don't you know?"

"And that is just the point. She is his half-sister! It is quite unnatural!"

Eyes widening, Clarissa turned to Lady Havers. Under the noise of the crowd, she asked, "Is he . . . are they . . . is this true?"

Lady Havers shook her head, setting the feathers on her turban to nodding. "It is true enough that Lady Byron has left him, my dear. And I have no doubt she was jealous of how he adores his half-sister, for she is a very sweet thing. But as to the rest, I do not know, and I do not wish to know.

"But, I will tell you this. Annabella Milbanke was a lovely, lovely girl who had no business setting her cap for Byron. Why, I do not believe she ever was really in love with him, but with how she thought he could be remade. And she ruined them all by marrying him and then running away when he acted up—as anyone knew he would, for he always does. She had only to stay with him, and they all could have come to Almack's tonight, and smiled and danced just like everyone. But, no, she had to make his wild ways a public scandal. She had to drag it all out before the world!

"And I hope you girls take this lesson to heart. When you marry, you had best be certain that you can live with a gentleman's faults, for you will ruin his life as well as your own if you cannot."

Lady Havers's footman came in just then with news that their carriage was at the door, and her ladyship herded them into the coach and four.

On the drive home, Clarissa sat on the leather seat, a warm brick at her feet and her thoughts churning, hardly listening to Lady Havers's gossip about the rest of the evening.

Could she be as willful as the beautiful Lady Byron had once been? Was she set on a course that would bring ruin to herself and others all because she did not want to compromise her dreams of passion and love?

The carriage stopped to leave Jane at the Prestons's on Half Moon Street, and then moved forward to Havers House, where it rocked to a standstill.

As the footman handed her out of the carriage, Clarissa remembered an odd tidbit from when her Aunt Maeve had been her governess and had instructed her, saying, "My dear girl, a compromise can be a concession, a necessary yielding. But it is terribly important to know when you are yielding for good reason, or when you are making a dangerous compromise that will ruin your principles."

And the trouble was, Clarissa thought, dutifully kissing her godmother good night and trudging up the stairs to her room, that she did not know if she ought to compromise and give up on finding a rake to reform—or if she ought to just let the rake compromise her and let it all work out however it would.

The bed curtains rattled on their rings, indicating Shadwick's presence. The sound of brass on wood echoed inside Wolviston's head like horses thundering through a cobbled stable yard.

Covering his closed eyes with a hand, Wolviston muttered, his mouth dry and stiff, "Shadwick, stop fussing. You're making the room spin."

"The room, m'lord, is quite stable. It is the brandy that is still spinning in your head. But I have brought you a restorative, m'lord."

Struggling to sit up, Wolviston had to pause with only his head raised and his elbows partly under him. "Will it stop this damn horse from kicking?"

"Kicking, m'lord?"

"In my skull." Slowly, Wolviston eased up until he sat in his four-poster bed with his pillows lumped behind him and his bedclothes wrapped around his sweaty body. Slitting open his eyes, he winced at sunlight that streamed in with unseemly brilliance, shafting like needles into his eyes.

"How does he do it, Shadwick? How does any rakehell do this, night after night, when the very next morning death would be a kinder end? Oh, damn, I wish the room would stop turning."

"I believe, m'lord, that repeated exposure hardens a man's constitution. And there may be some truth to it that the devil looks after his own. Now do drink this, m'lord."

Wolviston eyed the cup and saucer in his valet's hands. The man stood beside the bed, looking obscenely bright-eyed, his thinning hair brushed neatly back, his slight form tidy as a vicar's. The faint, bitter aroma of tea teased Wolviston's nose. His stomach rolled.

"What is it?" he asked.

"Tea, m'lord. Strong and heavily sugared. I learned to make it in Lord St. Albans's household."

Warily, Wolviston took the cup. He was pleased that his hands did not shake, for his stomach did, as did the rest of his insides. Never again, he vowed silently. Never again would he try to keep pace with St. Albans's devilment.

At least St. Albans now had no need to suspect he was anything but a hell-raiser, but the suspicion lay in his brain like a maggot that the entire night, St. Albans had been laughing inwardly at him. Wolviston had drunk more than he ought, had taken every pretty woman he saw into his arms, and had gambled recklessly. And it had been damn hard work. The entire time he had kept thinking of other places he would rather be and other things he would rather be doing.

Golden guineas spilled on a table seemed dull compared to the golden curls that had spilled into his fingers the other night in Lady Havers's conservatory. The kisses he had sampled all seemed lacking in passion. And the brandy had made his sullen mood darker.

He sipped Shadwick's steaming tea, lay still for a moment, and then thought he might want to live after all. The horse had almost stopped kicking behind his temples and the room started to settle.

Then a new pounding shook the room as heavy,

booted feet clomped up the stairs and burst into his room.

Wolviston's brothers crowded through the doorway, their hats askew, their faces red. They stood there, partly leaning on the door frame, gasping for air as if they had run a footrace.

Peter got his breath first and blurted out, "Evan, you'll never . . . guess who . . . we just about . . . ran into . . . on Oxford Street!"

Pressing hot fingers to throbbing temples, Wolviston glanced from one brother to the other, taking in their disheveled appearance while he waited for the dull thuds in his head to subside.

Peter's hat lay pushed back on his head, his coat flapped open, and his cravat looked as if it he had clawed it loose from his throat. The faint purple bruising around David's left eye told its own story of mischief gotten into at an earlier date.

Keeping his tone even so that it did not start his head aching more, Wolviston said, "Shadwick, bring more tea. And a beefsteak for David, if you please."

David's eyebrows arched in surprise. "That's awfully decent. But Peter and I ate hours ago."

"It's for your eye, not your stomach," Wolviston said. "And how, exactly, did you get your daylights darkened?"

Face reddening, David looked away, but Peter spoke up, his tone defensive. "He had to do something, Evan. You should have heard the scurrilous lies this fellow was telling about you and father, and about you being a dashed rake!"

Wolviston let out a soft groan and sank his head into his hand. Bad enough that he had dragged Clarissa into danger with his little escapade; now he had involved his brothers in ways that he would rather not. Well, he knew what must be done. He had known it for days, in fact, and had simply not wanted to admit it to himself. And while he might dread admitting the truth to them, he must, before they ended up fighting duels on his behalf.

Getting up, he dragged his red brocade robe over his nightshirt and stalked across the room to pull forward a pair of chairs for them. "Your defense of me is commendable, but I actually started that particular scurrilous story myself. Now sit down, be quiet, and if you ever repeat any of what I'm about to tell you without my permission you'll find out just how much a scoundrel I honestly can be."

When the boys were seated, with tea on a side table and a beefsteak for David to press to his swollen eye, Wolviston started talking.

As he spoke, he kept his attention focused on dressing, pulling on a pair of buckskin breeches and stripping off his nightshirt to drag on a shirt of lawn. It took every ounce of discipline not to give in to the urge to crawl back into his bed and tell them to go away. The room still tended to tilt, and a sour taste lay in his mouth, and not just from too much brandy.

Telling the story was like walking in mud—slow and exhausting. Halfway through, he knew he had done the wrong thing. They had grown utterly quiet, and he could not bear to watch their faces sober and their eyes widen in disbelief. Blindly, he gestured to one of the two waistcoats that Shadwick held out for his approval, and then he focused on trying to tie a decent knot in his cravat.

He skirted around how the pretense had all

started because of Clarissa Derhurst, for he was oddly reluctant to put her faults before his brothers for them to criticize. So he made the whole thing sound as if it started as a challenge between himself and Reggie—but only God knew where it would end.

When he finished, he stood in his shirtsleeves and stockinged feet.

"And I had better damn well not hear again that either of you has fought over my battered name," he said, his tone more aggressive than he had meant it. Brushed and shaved, he still felt as if he had been drug across gravel, inside out, for the better part of last night.

He drank his cold tea in one bitter swallow, and then braced himself to face his brothers' shocked scorn.

His brothers stared at him, their eyes owlishly large. Then Peter piped up, saying, "You—a rake?" He burst into a peal of laughter that left Wolviston scowling and his pride smarting.

"I don't see that it's that amusing."

"Amusing?" David said, grinning. "It's brilliant, that's what it is. But what the devil do you mean by not telling us about any of this until now?"

"Yes," Peter demanded, pushing back the locks of brown hair that kept spilling over his forehead and into his eyes. "Did you think we'd blow the gab on you?"

"Blow the gab? Just what circles have you been frequenting to be picking up thieves' slang?"

Peter's ears turned scarlet, but David waved aside the question. "Never mind that. What we need to do is figure out how we can help you now, for it's obvious you'll end in the suds without us."

Wolviston almost laughed himself. Less than a month ago, these two had set fire to a vicar's beehives. He could only imagine where their assistance would lead him in this farce.

Striving for as much severity as he could, he told them, "You can best help by staying out of fights on my behalf."

"You're going to need us," David insisted.

Glancing from one eager face to the other, Wolviston sensed that something had changed between them. Something intangible, but quite important. They no longer sat before him, stiff and uncomfortable, looking as if they rather dreaded having anything to do him. Instead, they sat up, eager-faced, eyes alight with interest, and looking at him with open admiration.

For an insane moment, a spark danced in him at the thought of his brothers actually in this with him. But no, that was not to be thought of. He could not, would not, jeopardize their reputations. Someone had to act responsibly. And he had for too long been that someone. He could not shrug off his duties like the rogue that he pretended to be.

"I do not need your aid," he insisted, and then sat down to pull on his riding boots.

David frowned, his brown eyes darkening. "Yes, you do. Because Mother's in town. We saw her shopping on Oxford Street."

Wolviston froze, his boot half on and his heart almost stopped. In that second, he wished he honestly did have a rakish scorn for the world. He could have used it. And then he simply muttered a heartfelt "Oh, hell!"

Having his mother in town made the whole matter

far more complicated—and far more imperative to resolve with as little fuss as possible. Devil take it, but Reggie might well be proved right. He might yet have to stage his own reform and marry the girl.

"Oh, hell," he muttered again, and then he stomped his boot onto his foot and turned to his brothers. "Right now, tell me everything you know about what Mother is doing in town."

Ten

It soon became apparent that neither David nor Peter knew more than that they had seen Lady Wolviston and her cousin and companion, Mrs. Martha Barstall, shopping on Oxford Street. When Wolviston asked if they might be mistaken, David said, much affronted, "We ought to know what our own mother looks like."

So Wolviston sent them away with a word to stay away from the shopping Mecca of Oxford Street. If Fanny, Lady Wolviston, was indeed in town, he would soon hear from her. But he would rather that she did not learn about David and Peter's latest adventures. She fretted over the boys, and if she heard that they had been sent down from school it could well result in her worrying herself into illness.

That afternoon a letter came rather late with the news, announcing Lady Wolviston's plans to visit London with a stay at Gordon's Hotel in Albermarle Street. Lady Wolviston wrote that she hoped her son might find time to see her, but that if he did not she would find the strength to somehow bear the disappointment.

Wolviston took the hint and dressed to pay a call on his mother.

He found her in a tidy parlor, looking much as she always had—which was, he thought, like a once richly painted porcelain cup that had been left in the sun until all the brightness had faded. Life had been hard for Fanny Fortesque.

She was a thin, elegant woman. Tall, with delicate bone structure, she had put off her deepest mourning blacks, and now wore a soft, dove-gray dress with black trim. He had not seen her hair in the past nine years, for she had taken to wearing a black lace cap, making it impossible to tell if her hair was still golden brown or if it had silvered. Deep lines creased her forehead, and pale blue eyes gazed up at him anxiously.

There had been times during the past decade when he feared that her worries might well drive her to an early grave. He had become an expert at shielding her from the boys' worst adventures. And at shielding them from her excessive cosseting. However, it would take rather more work to make certain she did not also learn of his own prank, playing a rake's role. At least, thank heavens, she had kept far enough from Society that she knew few who would carry tales to her about him.

She seemed rather more cheerful than he had seen her in quite some time, for she looked up as he entered and gave him a wan smile, putting her own cool and dry hand into his. "Evan, how good of you to call on us. But you look rather thin—are you well?"

He assured her that he was and turned to greet Cousin Martha, a stick of a woman with jet black hair and an unfortunate black fuzz on her upper lip. She was fond of purple and so inevitably wore the color, although it gave her skin an olive cast. The dress hung on her bony body, and she wore an orange-and-green Paisley shawl over her shoulders.

As customary, she did not look up from her knitting, but her needles clattered on as she mumbled an inaudible greeting that his mother interpreted. "Martha says she is also happy to see you. She is knitting a set of scarves for the boys, you know."

He had not known, and he did not care to ask why she should be knitting scarves with summer coming. Instead, he said, with a patient smile, "I am certain that David and Peter will keep them for years." Which they no doubt would, preferably in the bottom of a trunk.

Cousin Martha, as long as he had known her, which was all of his life, had always knitted. She had knitted for his father, for Uncle David—who David was named after—and for distant relatives whose names he could not remember. Everyone in the family had, at some point, been gifted with some of Martha's knitting—baby boots, mittens, even waistcoats. It had become a family obligation to wear that garment when she came visiting.

She had, however, proven to be the ideal companion for his mother. She did not find his mother's habitual worrying to be the least lowering—his mother had managed to drive two other companions into such depressions that they fled. And Cousin Martha hardly spoke a word, which was excellent in that his mother loved to talk.

No sooner had he sat down than she began to indulge that love.

For the first ten minutes, she mourned the loss of the London she had once known. The new roads were very nice, so much smoother now that they were paved, but now London seemed to push into the surrounding countryside. And she did not think the new gas lighting going in was really all that safe, and the new buildings seemed so austere and far too Greek-looking.

She went on to fret that even a stay of a few days in London would result in the dower house at Wolviston Abbey falling into ruin without her to manage the staff. And then she fussed over the boys for nearly a quarter of an hour, finally saying, "I had the most dreadful dream about them. A terrible one about them being caught in a tower by a dragon."

He would have laughed at the absurdity of it, but he knew that, for her, dreams always portended disaster. He could not blame her for thinking so. She had had a bad dream about an overturned carriage on the night before his father's nearly fatal accident. It had taken him three exhausting days back then to coax her back to a full night's sleep in her own bed. And months more to convince her that not every dream foretold the future.

So now, he offered a reassuring smile and said, "Yes, but there are very few dragons about these days. And you know it is only the very real dreams that have ever come true."

She frowned and pulled at the fringe on her shawl. "I do know that. But the dragon's fire seemed so very real. Perhaps I should stop at Cambridge and visit on the way home?"

Wolviston nearly choked on the tea she had poured him. "Visit? But the Easter term is going to start soon, and you know they'll be very busy then."

"Yes, but since it is between terms, is not now an ideal time to go and see how they do?"

"Well, umm, you would not want to interrupt what little time they have for enjoying some sports and time outside, now would you? Besides, I just heard from them and they seem to be doing quite well. And they have a great deal of reading up to do between terms. On mathematics."

"Do they? Oh, I do hope they are not studying too hard."

"Oh, I don't think you have to worry on that score," Wolviston said, his tone dry.

Lady Wolviston frowned. "And do you think they get enough to eat? They are still growing boys, and I do fear they will not be properly fed."

"I know just the thing, then. Why do you not send them some biscuits, or perhaps an entire basket from Fortnum and Mason?"

Her expression hesitant, Lady Wolviston worried the edging of the silk damask pillow next to her. "Well, if you think that is better, I supposed I could do so. Martha, shall we go there tomorrow?"

Martha muttered something and Lady Wolviston turned back to her son. "Martha thinks it a splendid notion, actually. She would like some of those lovely wafers they make to take home as well. Now, do take an extra cake, Evan, and tell me all the trouble you have been getting into."

Wolviston froze for a moment, thinking that she must have heard something. And then he realized that she had made a slight jest. He knew she had, for she gave him the smallest of smiles. It had been ages since she had even tried to do so. He relaxed, smiled back at her, and proceeded instead to question her about her plans.

He sent up a prayer of thanks when she said she did not feel up to any society as of yet. They had come because Cousin Martha needed some new yarns, and she thought it would be nice to perhaps pay a few morning calls to select old friends. If they felt up to it, and if the rain ever gave them a few days' respite, they might go for a stroll in Kensington Gardens to see the spring flowers, but nothing more dashing.

These quiet plans certainly made it less likely that she would encounter the boys—or anyone who might pass on any gossip about him. But Wolviston still vowed to warn David and Peter to keep to the masculine havens in town. If need be, he would send them away to Newmarket for a few days before the start of Easter Term and their return to Cambridge. He doubted they would mind being shuffled off to watch the spring racing meet.

He also promised to call on his mother again before she left town. And he told her firmly that she must ask him if she should like to do anything at all. Guilt stung him at her warm gratitude, for his motivation was to track her activities, not to provide her amusement. However, he promised himself he would buy her several new lace caps to atone for his poor intentions.

With that done, he had nothing better to do than waste an hour before he was due to dine with Reggie at White's. He walked about for most of that time, torn between the desire to see Clarissa again, and the common sense that urged him to stay away from her.

His desire he could explain as mere curiosity. There was not an hour that went by when he did not wonder what she had gotten up to lately. But he told himself that if he sought her out too soon after that kiss, he would be raising expectations in her. And he was not about to marry a girl just to ease his conscience, or hers, over a kiss.

He could certainly end his days as a rake right now with an abrupt exit from town, but that seemed a coward's way out. And to own the truth, he did not want to go. But what was he to do about Clarissa?

His steps took him to Berkley Square. He walked about the planted oval gardens in the center of the square once, hardly seeing the newly leafed trees.

Lord, he had invented more troubles than his mother ever would, he told himself. *Just go see the girl and get it over.*

Taking the front steps to Lady Havers's town house two at a time, he lifted the brass ring in the lion's mouth and rapped hard.

A moment later, Lady Havers's staid butler informed him that the ladies were not at home. He had to content himself with the thought that he would call on the ladies on the morrow.

However, the next few days brought their own occupations.

On the next day, just as he had dressed for a morning call, the boys appeared on his doorstep. They apologized, but said they needed an advance on their allowance. A large advance.

Slowly, tediously, Wolviston pulled the story from them.

They had lost a bet to see if a tame monkey could be made to climb the six Corinthian columns that fronted the Mansion House. Peter swore they had thought the bet would be easily won, but the monkey proved to be a non-starter, refusing even to start up the first column and thereby losing their bet by default.

Wolviston had listened to the story, a lecture forming in his head about such foolish wagers. Only somehow, what had come out when he began talking to them were recollections of his few weeks in London when he'd been nineteen and prime for anything. In particularly, he recounted a story about hiring an opera dancer to show up at Reggie's, complete with her sister's borrowed baby, to claim the babe as Preston's. Reggie's ensuing panic—and his efforts to try and explain to the dancer why he could not offer marriage, for his father would kill him on the spot—amused them for an hour. The other stories led into dinner at a nearby tavern.

In the end, he sent his brothers off with such a large amount of money in their pockets that he knew they would feel guilty if they lost it all on any other such nonsense. Then he left for the opera, where he was pledged to meet Reggie and some of his friends.

However, the entertainment seemed designed not to distract, but to torment. Every aria, every solo, made him think of the pleasure on Clarissa's face on the night of Lady Perry's musical evening. He stared up at Lady Havers's empty box the entire time, picturing Clarissa there, and quite certain that he was spending far more time thinking of her than she was in thinking of him.

The next day his mother wrote to say that since the day had dawned fair, would he be so kind as to

arrange a river outing to Hampton Court, for that
would be most pleasant. He did so, thinking it far
better to have her out of London for a day than run
the risk of her encountering the boys, Lady Havers,
or Clarissa. However, the day proved wearisome, with
Cousin Martha almost losing her knitting overboard.

His mother worried over the boat, fearing it would
leak. She worried that the sun would not stay out—
and it did cloud over several times during the day.
And then she began to worry over Evan as the oars-
men rowed them home, saying that she feared he
might fall out and drown. He told her cheerfully
that he was a strong swimmer, but her anxiety had
its effect on him, and he had his own nightmares
after he had gone to his bed, exhausted.

In the dream, he stepped into the small Saxon
chapel near Wolviston Abbey. Bare, cool gray stones
welcomed him with ancient peace and sanctuary.
Then he turned and found himself in the middle
of a wedding ceremony. All of London Society
seemed to crowd the cramped space. Barely able to
breathe for the press of people at his back, he struggled to move away from the pushing, which shoved
him into the groom's position, beside a veiled bride.

"It's not me you want," he tried to shout. But as
he did, the bride's white veil seemed to wrap around
him, suffocating, strangling. He began to flail at the
hands pushing him. His arms and legs tangled in
the gauzy veil, and when he could no longer move,
he heard a man's laughter and looked up to see
that the vicar was St. Albans. He turned then to see
his bride, but just before he glimpsed her face . . .

He woke, tangled in his sheets, sweating, his heart

pounding, the ache of his unvoiced protests still lodged in his throat.

It was a sign, he decided, rubbing a hand over sleep-befuddled eyes, that he had to see Clarissa. He had to sort things out with her and discover if that cursed kiss really had stirred any expectations in her. Then he would get his mother sent home, his brothers back to university, and he would settle down to some time for himself.

"You have been exceptionally quiet today," St. Albans remarked.

Clarissa looked up from the roses she had been arranging in Lady Havers's drawing room. She had offered to put his lordship's flowers in the vase, along with the other yellow roses he had brought the day before, and the day before that.

St. Albans had acted such a gentleman as of late that she had started to lose her nervousness around him. It helped, of course, to have Lady Havers, Jane, and Reggie close to hand. They, along with Mrs. Randall and Miss Randall, sat not three yards away, talking over the rumors that Lord Byron might quit England—some said for good. But, pretty as St. Albans's behavior had been, Clarissa could not but wonder if he really sought to improve his acquaintance with her, or simply hone his seduction techniques on her?

"I have been thinking," she said, picking up another rose. "How does one know what is a good compromise and what is one that is, well, a dangerous one? A bad one that jeopardizes all that one is and all that one wants?"

He pulled back a little. "Such deep waters. I had hoped you were thinking of me."

She smiled a little, and lifted a rose to her nose. The faint sweetness reminded her of her mother's rose garden and how intoxicating it smelled in spring.

After adding the rose to the other two dozen, she turned to him. "I am, in a fashion. You see, I do not know if you can give me what I want. And I do not know if I want what you can give. How do I find these answers?"

He picked up a rose and twirled it so that the faint spice of its scent drifted across the small distance between them. "There is but one way I know for a man and a woman to gauge if they fit each other's needs."

Her cheeks heated a little. "For shame. I speak of the heart, and I believe you speak of the body."

"The two are not separate items, Miss Derhurst. The heart often follows where the body leads."

"Does it? But I have heard some say that you do not have a heart. Or perhaps it ought to be said that you have a collection of hearts, all from ladies unwise enough as to give theirs into your careless hands."

He smiled at her, one of his rare true smiles. "I have a heart. I certainly hear it beat when you step near and my pulse quickens."

She gave a laugh. "You promised me no flattery and here you are, already breaking your vow."

"That is what I am best at," he said, a hand over his heart.

She gave him a sideways glance, uncertain, as usual, if he was telling the truth or teasing. Before she could ask which it was with him, Lady Havers's butler, Bentley, knocked at the door and then entered with a letter upon a silver tray.

"Pardon me, my lady. This missive just arrived for Miss Derhurst and it is marked urgent," he said with a deep bow.

Clarissa came over at once. She picked up the letter, snapped the wax seal, spread open the folded sheet, and scanned the hurried scrawl. Then she gave a small shriek. "The baby's come! My uncle has an heir and I've a new cousin!"

Lady Havers gave a shriek as well and jumped to her feet, and then it seemed as if everyone was on their feet and smiling and talking all at once. Lady Havers caught Clarissa in a warm embrace, then Clarissa turned to hug Jane tightly, and then somehow she turned and she was in St. Albans's arms.

She stiffened, but he released her at once, his smile wicked, and she thought it had not been all that alarming. Then he glanced toward the doorway, a smug look on his face.

Clarissa's stare followed his. Her heart gave a skip as she saw Wolviston standing in the open doorway, his hat and walking stick still in his hands. Then her smile faded and her eyes widened in awe as she took in Wolviston's brooding glare and his tensed shoulders. She had never seen a man look more dangerous—and it sent a rather delectable shiver through her.

In the instant when he saw St. Albans's arms around Clarissa, Wolviston's vision narrowed and a fire engulfed him from the inside. Blood roared in his ears. He wanted only to walk across the room and drag Clarissa out of St. Albans's reach—and then throttle the damn fellow.

Sanity returned a second later.

Lady Havers stepped forward, babbling something Wolviston could not hear for the pounding in his ears. The touch of her hand on his arm reminded him, however, that he stood in her house, in polite company, and could not act on the violence that burned in him.

He forced a smile, gave his hat and stick to Lady Havers's butler, and said something inane about having arrived at an awkward moment. "I heard Clarissa—Miss Derhurst's cry, you see, and . . ."

"Leapt to the rescue?" St. Albans finished, his voice mocking. "But there is only a letter from home to slay."

Wolviston locked stares with St. Albans and a silent tension crackled in the air. Reggie Preston eased it, stepping forward and asking Lady Havers if the news of Lord Rothe's son and heir seemed good cause to open some champagne.

At once, Lady Havers issued orders for refreshments. Reggie engaged St. Albans with a question about when he planned to marry and get his own heir, Jane turned to talk to Mrs. Randall and her daughter, and Wolviston found himself able to step aside with Miss Derhurst for a private word.

"Why do you encourage him?" he muttered, his jaw still tight and aching.

Indignation sparked in her eyes. "Do you mean Lord St. Albans? Unlike some gentlemen, he needs no encouragement to be social. He likes to come and pay his compliments to myself and my god-mama."

"So it's his flattery that has turned your head? I thought you had more sense than to believe mere honeyed words."

"Honeyed words sit far better with me than does neglect. But I suppose you have been far too busy with your other affairs." She bit off the rest of her words. She had not meant to say anything to him about his absence. She had meant to act as if that kiss between them had never happened. If he could, then so could she.

But the hurt of his turning away had seeped out, and now she wanted both to laugh for the wonderful news from home and lash out for how miserable she felt.

"Actually, family matters have occupied my time," he said.

She arched her brows and eyed him. Strained lines lay at the corners of his eyes and shadows smudged his eyelids. He looked tired. The absurd impulse to smooth his lined forehead rose in her, and she stamped it down. The next move had to be his, for she was not going to set her cap for any man who did not want her.

Instead, she said with a smile, striving for a calm she did not feel, "Ah, here is the champagne. Will you have some?"

She moved away to help Lady Havers order glasses into everyone's hands.

Then Lady Havers raised a crystal goblet, sunlight sparkling in the pale, bubbling wine. "To . . . oh, dear, what is his name?"

Blushing, Clarissa realized she had not even taken note of her new cousin's name. She put down her glass and had to fumble with the letter, then said,

"He is to be christened after my father. So he is to be Philip . . . ah, here it is . . . Philip Andrew Clarence Douglas."

"To Philip Andrew Clarence Douglas Derhurst," Lady Havers said.

They all drank, and then Bentley filled everyone's glasses again, and the talk turned to christening gifts.

It was St. Albans who glanced around and proposed an afternoon shopping expedition for suitable presents.

Inwardly cursing, Wolviston glanced at the man, wondering if the Earl had a pact with the devil to know that the last thing in the world that he wanted was to throw Clarissa anywhere near shops where she might meet his mother.

Mrs. Randall excused herself and her daughter, saying they had other calls to pay. She was obviously bursting to convey the news around town about Lord Rothe's new heir. But the other ladies at once began to lay plans for the shops that must be visited.

Catching Reggie's eye, Wolviston managed to pull him aside. "We can't let St. Albans take them shopping."

"His reputation is bad, old son, but no one's going to quibble over him squiring ladies about in public."

"Damn St. Albans. It's my mother that's the risk. You know she's in town, and the last thing I need is them all meeting up over gewgaws, or ices at Gunter's!"

Reggie stared at him. "Good God! I hadn't thought of that. But aren't you being a touch arrogant, old son, to think they'd talk of you if they did meet?"

"You've met my mother, Reg. Her two topics are imminent disasters and her sons. She knows Lady Havers. And do you think Clarissa will not start in with a dozen questions?"

Reggie drained his champagne. "I suppose she will. Never met a female more likely to blurt out things. But what the devil can you do about it?"

"It's what you can do." Wolviston quickly sketched a plan for Reggie to stop and visit his mother.

"And where will you be while I am so busy?" Reggie demanded.

"Shopping," Wolviston said, his voice grim.

Reggie frowned, considering this. Of the choices offered, an afternoon spent with Fanny, Lady Fortesque, seemed an ordeal, right enough, but far less a one than having to spend the afternoon looking over baby clothes. The only thing he would miss, he decided, would be seeing the boredom on St. Albans's face.

The shopping expedition soon resolved itself into two groups. Lady Havers's landau would take her ladyship, Jane, and Lord Wolviston, while Lord St. Albans would take up Clarissa in his curricle, which he had driven over for his visit. Wolviston disliked the arrangement, but he hid his displeasure under a warm smile, for he would not do anything to make Jane Preston feel as if he found her company in the least lacking.

So it was that Clarissa had to watch with tight lips and a fixed smile as Lord Wolviston handed Jane into the landau, making her laugh with something he said, his grip strong on Jane's arm and steadying on her waist.

Turning to Lord St. Albans, Clarissa tried to dis-

tract herself. She began to chatter away about her
family, about how her little cousin Sophie must be
thrilled with a new brother, and all the news from
home that she had read. She babbled on until a
bored look glazed St. Albans's eyes. He pulled up
his team before Grafton House on New Bond Street
with as close to an expression of relief as she had
ever seen on his face.

The first order of the day was to buy material to
send to Yorkshire for an elegant christening gown.

Clarissa and the other ladies spent a pleasant hour
admiring laces, selecting suitable ribbons, and de-
ciding whether white or oyster was to be preferred.

During that time, Wolviston found one grudging
thing to respect in his rival—St. Albans seemed to
have endless patience with female shopping habits.
The man sounded utterly sincere when he admired
selections, praised the ladies' tastes, and offered colors to match.

Finally, the material had been selected, cut,
folded, and wrapped. Ribbons were chosen—in pale
blue and also in a matching oyster. Lady Havers
added an elegant bit of red silk for herself, which
she simply could not resist. Then the gentleman
bowed them out into the street again.

Once there, St. Albans said to Wolviston, his voice
pitched so as not to be heard over the traffic, "Quite
the ordeal, is it not?"

Wolviston shrugged off his boredom. "I've been
through worse."

St. Albans smiled. "You might yet be through
worse today. It seems that Mr. Preston is across the
street, trying to catch your glance and looking
rather grim about something."

Looking up, Wolviston spotted Reggie. His face was almost as red as his hair and scrunched up with a desperate anxiety. He raised empty hands, palms up.

"What the devil?" Wolviston muttered.

Reggie found a break in the flow of carriages, wagons, and riders and sprinted across.

"Why, Mr. Preston," Lady Havers said, smiling at him. "I thought you had a call to pay."

Reggie gave a small bow. "I did." He locked eyes with Wolviston. "Found they were out—shopping, it seems."

"Well, never mind that, where to next?" Lady Havers said as her carriage halted from the circles the driver had been making to keep the horses from chilling in the brisk air. She turned to allow the footmen to assist her in entering.

Wolviston exchanged a glance with Reggie, silently offering up a prayer that the ladies might tire soon and that this day would end.

And then he watched Fate laugh at his hopes as his mother alighted from a hired hackney that had pulled to a halt just behind Lord St. Albans's curricle and pair.

Eleven

Turning his back to his mother, Wolviston glanced at the other ladies who stood on the pavement, still discussing where they ought to go next. He had to get them out of here. Fast.

"Reggie, where the devil can we get them in short order?" Wolviston muttered.

Reggie's face knotted, and then he snapped his gloved fingers. "Got it. The Soho Bazaar. Just the place to look for fripperies and such. What do you say, Lady Havers, shall we have a go at that new bazaar in Soho Square?"

"Yes, let us do so at once," Wolviston said. He could not afford to give the ladies time to quibble. Cousin Martha had already alighted from the hired hack as well. "Reggie, do you mind going with St. Albans to show him the way? Ladies?"

Jane and Clarissa exchanged a mystified look, but Wolviston already had hold of Jane's hand. He all but tossed her, and then Clarissa, into the landau. Jumping in after them, he gave the driver the direction to Soho Square.

Reggie at once linked his arm with St. Albans's and started to lead him down the street, away from

Lady Wolviston. St. Albans pulled away and glared at him. "My curricle is the other way, Preston."

"Ah, so it is," Reggie said, ducking his hat low over his face as Lady Wolviston walked past him, her stare fixed on the doors to Grafton House.

Wolviston let out the breath he had been holding as he watched his mother pass Reggie without a glance. It had been well over a year since she had last seen Reggie. However, there had been the chance that she might recognize Reggie's distinctive ginger coloring.

The knot in Wolviston's shoulders relaxed as he saw disaster averted. He had taken the backwards-facing seat in the landau, next to Miss Preston, and now he turned back to the ladies in time to catch Clarissa's puzzled stare. She must think him mad to be carrying them off with such urgency. She looked away at once, and Wolviston turned his attention to Lady Havers, who chattered on about the bargains that she had heard could be found in the Soho Bazaar.

Lady Havers soon gave them all the background any of them could want on the bazaar.

It had only just been opened that year by a Mr. Trotter to help the widows and daughters of men who had died in the recent wars, a noble cause that Lady Havers thrilled to. The bazaar occupied the northwest corner building in the Square; vendors sold their wares in stalls set up along two floors, offering gloves, lace, jewelry—almost anything that might be crafted for sale.

It was, in short, a paradise for Lady Havers, whose eyes lit with a rapacious glow when they entered.

Clarissa at once found a delightful quilt, done in

white on white and the perfect size, she judged, for a baby's cradle. Lady Havers bought herself a fan, a pair of gloves, and two woolen Paisley shawls; she then decided she would make presents of the shawls, sending one to Lady Rothe and one to Clarissa's mother. Reggie helped Jane to buy a set of carved wooden toy soldiers, and St. Albans bought a riding whip, saying it was the sort of present a boy would grow into.

Wolviston found nothing to urge him to part with his money. In fact, he found it impossible to concentrate on buying anything. The near encounter with his mother had left him glancing over his shoulder, watching for her slight gray figure and Cousin Martha's purple gown. Half his attention focused on looking out for trouble, and the other half fixed on St. Albans's annoying attention to the ladies.

The ladies—and Clarissa in particular—seemed to enjoy the man's company. They smiled at his droll observations of other shoppers—of fashion's absurdities, and Wolviston clenched his teeth into a stiff smile. They asked for St. Albans's opinion on prices, and Wolviston scowled as he saw that even Jane Preston dimpled and smiled shyly when St. Albans insisted on paying a boy to carry her packages back to the carriage.

The man's damnable charm turned himself and Reggie into unnecessary backdrops. St. Albans appeared at Clarissa's side to lend his arm when the group moved forward to the next stall. He advised the ladies, flirted with them, and by comparison, Wolviston felt himself to be as lively as one of the wooden soldiers Jane had bought.

As they started back to the carriage, Clarissa

stopped to admire a spray of silk flowers. Lady Havers demanded Lord St. Albans's opinion on an embroidered handkerchief while the Prestons moved forward, and Wolviston at last had the opportunity to offer Clarissa his arm.

She glanced up, her cheeks coloring to the hue of summer peaches, and then she laid her gloved hand on his sleeve. A strained silence settled between them, however, as they followed the others down the stairs and back to the entrance.

He wished for the life of him that he had the right to tell her not to be taken in by St. Albans's act. He knew what the fellow was. He ought to, for he'd been to some of the worst hells in London with the man. But what could he say without sounding an utter hypocrite? He, not St. Albans, had stolen that kiss from her, after all.

"Lovely weather, is it not?" Clarissa said at last.

He nodded and muttered an agreement.

"Do you think it might rain again soon, though?"

"Quite," he said.

She halted and glanced at him, a small frown tugging her dark brows together over her blue eyes. "The least you might do is pay heed to my small talk. I have very little of it, so it wears out altogether too soon to be ignored."

Glancing down at her, he could not resist the smile that tugged at the corner of his mouth. "I beg your pardon, but I was wishing everyone else in this expedition to perdition so that I might have a word with you in private."

"Oh," she said, her eyes wide.

She took up his arm, and they began walking again. Clarissa slowed her steps so that they fell behind the others a little. She could not help but think of the last time they had spoken in private. He had kissed her then. Of course, he could not kiss her in such a public place as this. She could almost wish it were not so public.

"May I ask you a rather personal question?" Wolviston asked.

She slanted a glance up at him from under the brim of her bonnet, a stylish thing with a poke brim that Wolviston could have consigned to the devil for how it too often hid her face. "If you do not ask, I may have to go back to my small talk and that would bore us both back into silence."

"Then I will ask instead why it is that you seem to want a devil of a husband? You have two of the worst fellows in London—myself and St. Albans— paying you court, when instead you could be encouraging any number of respectable gentlemen. Is it that you want some fellow who, like the supposed knights of old, will prove his love to you?"

She wrinkled her nose. "You make me sound as if I want gentlemen to jump through hoops for my favor, but that is not at all the case."

"Then what do you want? I'd very much like to know why a bad reputation is so important to you."

"You will think me silly if I tell you."

"I already think that now, so you may as well tell me more, and then perhaps I shall change my mind about you."

Clarissa glanced up at him. His expression seemed quite serious. His eyes had darkened to pewter gray and he regarded her with such an intensity that her face warmed from it. She turned her stare to the stalls nearest her side, looking at the colored lace and the vendors' eager faces.

She did not like that Wolviston thought her silly, and somehow it seemed the most important thing in the world that he understand her reasons.

"Have you ever wanted something so much that you would do almost anything for it?" she asked.

"Yes," he said.

"And have you ever known that you needed something in your life—something that might keep all your worst faults from ruining yourself?"

He did not answer for a moment, and she glanced up at him. He looked straight ahead, his expression unreadable and his stare distant. And then he said, "A month ago, I would not have known what you meant. But now . . . yes, I can see how our faults often fashion traps we cannot seem to escape."

She nodded. "Yes. That is it exactly. It is not so much that I want a bad man's love. It is more that I need a great love. A great passion. And is that not what a rake is known to excel at?"

"I see. And, of course, a gentleman cannot possibly offer you such passion," he said, his mouth twisting down and the question made into a statement.

He almost wanted to take her by the shoulders and show her that dull gentlemen could manage a fairly good amount of passion. But, damnably, he was too much the gentleman to do so.

She stopped at a stall to admire a delicate lace trim made in the shape of butterflies. "My mother would love this. She adores pretty things. She was an even greater beauty than I, and she, too, has always needed a great deal of love. But she . . ."

Clarissa broke off, unable to say the truth, even to him.

"But she what?" he prompted.

The voices of vendors offering their wares seemed to fade. The faint smell of pastries, baking at the back of the building, carried to Clarissa, a smell of home almost. And the memory rushed back.

She was ten again, with her face framed between the stair rails. Rosewood pressed cool on her cheek. The sweetness of beeswax and the warmth of the hall fire mixed their scents. Anticipation danced in her stomach, and then a cold draft of wind brushed across her face as the front door opened. Her parents swept in, their colored evening cloaks swirling, their voices raised, and her excitement changed to dread.

Her father's voice, harsh and bitter, cut with the bite of steel. "It's a simple question. Answer me. How many times have you betrayed me?"

Her mother, trembling, almost crying, swung around, her hand cracking across his face. Then she stepped back, her face pale. "I should have married for love. And then I would not have to hunt for it elsewhere."

Clarissa had turned and run back to her room then, and had buried her face in her pillow. And the next morning her parents had been smiling, seeming quite normal, other than for the tension that lay between them like a sword balanced on its tip.

Blinking, Clarissa tried to shake off those frightened feelings which still confused her. She swallowed the lump in her throat. Her parents had loved each other, in their own ways. But it had not been strong enough, nor deep enough, to make them truly happy. She would not make that mistake in her own life.

"What happened, Clarissa?" Wolviston asked, his voice soft.

She let out a breath and sorted laces without seeing what she had in her hands. "Nothing, really. I grew up too like my mother. That is all. I think she loved my father in her own way—she certainly fell apart when he died. And he . . . well, I suppose he loved her after his own fashion. But Papa was a respectable gentleman."

"With a wife who needed far more?"

She looked up at Wolviston, saw the sympathy in his eyes, and had to look away before his pity undid her.

Forcing a cheerful tone, determined to show that such old wounds did not matter to her, for she could take care of herself, she said, "Quite. And I am just like my mama. My father even told me so. The last time I saw him, in fact. It was just before I got into the carriage to go to school, he took my face in his hands and then he said that I was just like my mother and that I must have a care to learn to school myself. Only I have never really known how to do so, as you must know by now."

The smile she turned up to him carried a hint of defiance as well as hurt.

A chill chased down Wolviston's spine. What a thing to say to a girl—to fix in her mind that she would follow her mother's path, making the same mistakes. He heard the fear that lay under her words, he saw it lurking behind the smile she put on for him.

"And now you no doubt know that I am silly, but I don't care. I am not going to become like my mother. I am going to marry for love—for real love, and passion, and fire, and . . ."

"And the reform of your rake?" Wolviston said dryly.

Clarissa's chin took on a stubborn tilt. "Love makes its own reforms to a person's character. I shall not make any demands at all."

"That sounds as if it might be a difficult promise for you to keep."

She stopped. They stood almost at the entrance to the bazaar and from here they could see the others waiting for them. Other shoppers brushed past, and carriages clattered along the square, the brass on the leather harness jingling.

Clarissa glared up at him, obviously stung by his criticism. Then she said, her tone defiant, "Perhaps love will make its own reforms on me as well."

He smiled at her. He could not help it. Lord, she became as prickly as a hedgehog when anyone dared point out the least possible flaw in her.

He tucked her hand into his arm again and led her toward Lady Havers's open landau. "I hope you do not reform too much, Miss Derhurst, for it would make the world a far less interesting place."

On the drive home, Clarissa pondered Lord Wolviston's comment. Had he been teasing her? What had he meant *the world would be less interesting*? Was that a compliment? Or had he been laughing at her? She suspected the latter, and it made her wish that she had had something very cutting and witty to say in reply. But the sad truth was that it would take two days or more to think up just the right thing that she ought to have said.

Clarissa's deep sighs drew Lady Havers's concern, but Clarissa at once reassured her ladyship that it was no more than a touch of wistful longing to see her new cousin.

Her words brought an awareness that there was indeed a hollow ache inside her. How nice it would be to throw her arms around her mother. And to see little Sophie—who must have grown so much in the past three months. And to sit in the garden with her Aunt Maeve and have a long talk about . . . well, about everything. With a sharp ache in her chest, Clarissa realized that she even missed her uncle's stern face and his all-too-dry sense of humor.

So, in the hall, as they took off their bonnets, Clarissa suggested, "Perhaps, Lady Havers, I ought to make a short visit home? Just for a few days. For Easter perhaps?"

With her bonnet dangling from her fingers, Lady Havers turned a look of shocked dismay on Clarissa. "But, my dear, the trip to York could take up to a week! Why, you might even end up spending Easter Sunday in some remote hamlet, far from any decent church. Have I not kept you well entertained that you wish yourself at home now?"

Stung with regret for her words, Clarissa twisted her bonnet ribbons in her fingers until Lady Havers's butler took it from her. "It is not that, but . . ."

"And what would Dorothy think if you go home with the season barely started in earnest?" Lady Havers started pacing, her steps agitated. "Without even an engagement in the planning? Oh, your mother will think I have failed her, and you as well! She will—quite justly—blame me for not being a good enough godmother as to know how to take you around properly."

Tears welled up in Lady Havers's light brown eyes. She began to search herself for a handkerchief. "But, I suppose, if you are set on going home and leaving me alone again, I will have to bear with the disappointment and misery your departure will leave in your wake."

"Please, your ladyship," Clarissa said, coming to her side and offering her own lawn handkerchief.

Lady Havers took the tiny square of fabric and dabbed at her eyes. "All I have done, I have done for your pleasure, you know. But, if you wish to leave me, you must do as you must."

Guilt for making her ladyship so miserable tightened in Clarissa's chest. "Please, do not cry. I . . . I really do not wish to go home."

Sniffling, Lady Havers peered over the top of her handkerchief, her eyes watery and already beginning to swell. "You . . . you do not? Really?"

"How could I when you have been so kind to me? It is just that . . . well, with a new cousin, I thought I should . . ."

"Oh, I see now. You thought you might go and be of aid to your aunt. But, my dear, trust me, you would just find yourself in the way. You would be ignored. Baby boys always do leave the girls ignored. It was just so in my own home when I was growing up."

"Ignored," Clarissa repeated, a hollowness inside her. Yes, how stupid of her. Why would anyone wish to have her at home when they had a new baby to make a fuss over? She had been selfish, thinking only that perhaps her family would be glad to see her. But her aunt would be busy with the baby—and so would her mother. And it was not as if she was a baby herself and needed their care, now was it?

After dabbing her eyes dry, Lady Havers linked her arm with Clarissa's. "But you shall not be ignored here, my dear. No, indeed. And I vow that the next few months will flash past in an instant, for you shall be so engaged in merriment. Now, let us take tea and you shall tell me what you would most like to do. And I shall not be in the least bit teased if you tell me you would rather attend a masked ball instead of Almack's."

With a determined smile, Clarissa allowed herself to be led into the first floor drawing room. She listened to a long list of diversions—excursions to Vauxhall gardens and its fireworks, picnics to Box Hill, watercolor exhibitions at the Royal Academy, a tour of Carlton House and the Prince's art collection, tickets to the Lyceum Theater, and waltzing parties to learn the latest steps.

And then Lady Havers sat upright. "Oh, but there is nothing so wonderful as a ball, now is there?"

Clarissa blinked. "But you held one just last month for me. Will it not be rather expensive?"

"Oh, of course it will. That is why they are so much fun. But we must hold one, in any case, in honor of your new cousin. And no one was really in London six weeks ago, now were they? Oh, I must have Bentley send out invitations at once, for we must invite everyone who is anyone. And then, at the end of June, when heat is unbearable and that horrible stench from the Thames closes Parliament, why that will be soon enough for you to visit your family. In fact, I shall come with you, for I must escort you home, and Yorkshire shall be so charming in June. So much cooler. Oh, you are a dear to think of this most excellent scheme!"

Clarissa smiled and said a weak thank you, and that she should at least write a letter home. But when she settled into the cozy room at the back of the house, which overlooked the garden and served as Lady Havers's study, she sat there, blank of mind and soul.

From the rosewood desk, she stared out into the small back garden to Lady Havers's house, trying to think what she might write home other than that she missed them all.

She could not write how she found Lord Wolviston so utterly attractive, with those wonderfully broad shoulders, and those soulful gray eyes which made her say things to him that she ought not. So, she wrote of Lord St. Albans and the yellow roses that he sent her every day. She wrote of the plans for a ball, and she wrote bright nonsense and hoped she did not actually sound as miserable as she felt.

Oh, bother, why must she have to choose at all between her suitors? Why could not one of them make passionate love to her and declare his mended ways?

She would just have to provide them better opportunities for doing so, she supposed. And that was definitely not something to put in a letter for home. With a firm flourish, she signed her letter, folded it, and addressed it.

There, she felt better already. She would do as

Lady Havers said and would become too busy to miss anyone at all.

The next ten days passed in a blur of activity. Lady Havers changed the invitation list twice before Bentley managed to have the page boys escape from the house to deliver them. Her ladyship ordered a dozen cases of champagne, then changed her mind, thinking to serve punch, and then decided she ought to serve wine, and then it was back to champagne again. She ordered masses of flowers, then decided to drape the ballroom in blue and white instead, to make it look like heaven. But when they went to Lady Sydney's fete, her ladyship had done just that, and so another decorating scheme had to be thought of.

Then there was Easter, which came late that year. Lady Havers took Clarissa to hear service at St. George's, and, of course, that meant new gowns and hats for such a fashionable congregation. Time had to be found to fit new ball gowns and day gowns, and by Easter, Clarissa was so worn that she nearly shamed herself by yawning during the rather dry sermon.

Before and after Easter, St. Albans visited every morning, more often than not taking Clarissa with him. She was thankful to escape with him. And if it was not St. Albans calling on her, it was Wolviston who came to compete for her attention.

They were, both of them, starting to be a bit silly about it.

If St. Albans sent her roses, Wolviston sent orchids. If she rode in the park with Wolviston, then St. Albans insisted that she allow him to drive her in his black curricle.

And from the stories she heard, the gentleman did not let this rivalry stop there.

Reggie told her of how St. Albans, when he had seen Wolviston bidding on a hunter for sale at Tattersall's, had bid against him, finally buying the horse for eight hundred pounds—four times its value. She also heard other tales, of hard gambling at less-than-reputable establishments.

It seemed, she thought, her temper shortening with them, that instead of inspiring either man to reform, she brought out their worst. Well, enough was enough of that. She would show them quite publicly at the ball that she would not allow herself to become a sport for them. She wanted one reformed rake, not two unrepentant sinners.

"I hear Wolviston's family is in town."

The Earl of St. Albans turned slightly toward the gentleman's voice. In the quiet of the paneled reading room in White's, he shifted behind his ironed copy of *The London Times* so that he could better hear.

"Family?" said a second voice, and then followed it with a huge sneeze, induced, St. Albans decided, by taking too greedy a pinch of snuff.

"His brothers. Two of 'em," the first voice answered, and St. Albans identified the lazy tone as belonging to a stuffy major who had made his money from the East India Company's tea trade. "Cut from the same cloth, by what I hear. Got sent down from university for some devilment. Mother's in town as well. Wearing mourning gray and not accepting invitations."

"I wouldn't either, with such relations about. Now you mention it, I heard there was a devil of a row between Wolviston and his brothers. Nearly came to blows, did they not, at some gaming hell?"

The major and his friend moved away, taking their gossip with them, leaving St. Albans with his own thoughts.

He was amused at how the story of the brothers' meeting had grown from the simple encounter he had witnessed to blows being exchanged. By the end of another week, a duel would have been fought in secret, at the very least. How utterly predictable the world could be.

Folding his newspaper, St. Albans rose.

He spent every morning in his club. He ate his breakfast—toast, strong black coffee, and thin slices of ham. Then he read his paper. He never had company. He hated to talk before he had had his second cup of coffee. Besides, the only man he had ever called friend did not care for London. So he did without company in the mornings.

But he was rich enough to have many acquaintances and bad enough to have many more enemies, and they were always far more amusing to have near to hand for entertainment later in the day. Wolviston seemed destined to fall into that latter category, for St. Albans was now certain that the man was an utter fraud. He hated frauds. But the man's pose had won him the golden Clarissa's interest. And that galled even more.

In the carpeted hall, St. Albans snapped his fingers and a liveried servant hurried forward with St. Albans's hat and York-tan gloves. He tossed the man a stray coin from his pocket, then strode out into the crisp spring air. A shaft of brilliant sunlight pierced the gathering clouds.

Wolviston had gone from being an irritation to a serious rival. The man had, St. Albans knew, kissed the girl. But he had not done more. That alone had left St. Albans certain that Wolviston was a fraud, and yet he had no proof to lay before the fair Clarissa. No evidence that might harden her heart against the damn fellow.

Stopping, St. Albans glared at a pair of brewers, carrying a keg between them. They crossed to the other side of the street to avoid him, but St. Albans watched them without any real interest.

How was he to get rid of this Wolviston so he could claim Clarissa for himself?

That question lay in his mind like those ridiculous carved wooden puzzles that his maiden Aunt Saffie had always been putting together. St. Albans had solved those easily enough. At eight, he had simply tossed them all into the fire. He'd already been an earl for eight years by then, and that was his first taste that he could do anything he wanted, for no one ever said a word to him about those cursed puzzles.

Pity that Wolviston could not be so easily gotten rid of.

But could this information on Wolviston's family prove useful?

He strode forward, scowling, his mood dark. What irritated most was the knowledge that he would have shrugged off the affair and let Wolviston play his game, if the fellow had not become such an obstacle to his own fascination with Miss Derhurst.

As elusive as a golden fish swimming in liquid

bliss, she taunted and teased and tempted. He had almost forgotten how exhilarating the chase could be. He had thought her well caught twice before, only to have her slip away from him. Each time, her escape fired a growing hunger. He wanted to know what she might be like once her appetites were awakened. He wanted to show her—and prove to himself—that there really was no true innocence in the world.

And for that he needed her to come to him.

St. Albans began to swing his cane as he walked. One way or another, he would have to put a spoke in Wolviston's plans. And he would have to make certain that when he did so, such a spoke left the headstrong Clarissa willing to run into his own arms.

"You are not staying in town," Wolviston said again, without slowing his steps. "You are going to Newmarket, and then back to Cambridge for the start of next term."

Scowling, Peter scuffed his boots along the pavement of Piccadilly, while David glared back at Wolviston.

"You want us out of the way," David said, his tone sulky.

"That is exactly where I want you. The last two days of rain have left Mother thinking how snug the dower house is at Wolviston, and if the bad weather holds, she'll quit town and we can all breathe easier."

Peter looked up at the clouds overhead, and then back to his oldest brother. "But we can't help you from bloody Newmarket!"

Wolviston stopped and looked from one brother to the other. "I never thought I should have to badger you two to attend a racing meet. What must I do, bribe you to go?"

David brightened. "You could let us stay."

"We could keep an eye on Mother for you. You know, follow her about to keep her from encountering someone you don't want her to meet."

"I don't want her to meet the two of you. And, if you meet, do you want her spasms on your conscience? You know very well if she finds out you've been sent down, she'll demand you be taken out of university and saddled with tutors back at the Abbey where she can keep you both on a very short leash. For your own good!"

Peter let out a deep sigh and David frowned. Wolviston knew that he had gotten through to them at last and he softened his tone. "Look here, I've started off on the wrong foot with all this. I should have realized you are far too old, both of you, for me to order you about." David straightened and pride glimmered in Peter's dark eyes at that comment, but Wolviston continued as if he had not noticed their reactions. "If I make it a request, will you please quit town until the end of next term?"

David rubbed at his struggling side-whiskers and Peter, looking uncertain and even younger than his seventeen years, fiddled with the brass buttons on his coat.

For a moment, Wolviston thought he had at last made them see sense, and then a voice from the street interrupted, calling out his name. He turned to see St. Albans smoothly halt his team of matched grays. Irritatingly, Wolviston had to look up to see the fellow.

Peter gaped at the glossy black curricle and the pair of high-strung grays in harness. "I say that's a bang-up rig."

St. Albans lifted an eyebrow and gave him a dismissive glance that had Peter turning red to his ears. The Earl then turned to Wolviston. "These must be the brothers I've been hearing about. Do you know that you all fought a duel yesterday—swords at dawn?"

He did not want to be amused, but Wolviston could not stop the smile that crooked his mouth. "Then you had better take care, had you not, St. Albans? If we do not hesitate to run each other through, no man is safe from us."

Both Peter and David grinned.

Handing the reins to his groom, St. Albans stepped down from his curricle. "Well, Wolviston, are you going to present me? I hate to duel with someone I don't know."

A touch reluctant to have his brothers known to a man such as St. Albans, Wolviston made the introductions. But he soon realized that their time in town had done his brothers good service. They looked impressed by St. Albans—who would not be with such horses, a title, and that damnable charm. But they only gave St. Albans a respectful and wary greeting, then looked to Wolviston for their cue.

Smiling, St. Albans eyed the brothers. "You are coming to Lady Havers's ball, are you not? Oh, you simply must. Her ladyship would be delighted to meet you—as would Miss Derhurst."

"Ball? What ball?" Peter asked.

David frowned at him, then turned to St. Albans. "Thank you, but we have not had an invitation."

"Oh, I will speak to her ladyship and make certain she knows you are in town. She already knows your mother is here."

Wolviston's head snapped up and his eyes narrowed. "What the devil do you know of my mother, sir?"

"Me, sir? Nothing." Turning away, St. Albans climbed into his curricle, then glanced back and his smile widened. "But do ask Lady Havers how she enjoyed taking tea with me at Gordon's Hotel."

With a crack of his whip over his team, St. Albans set off at a brisk trot.

Muttering a curse, Wolviston decided it honestly would be pistols at dawn if St. Albans had done anything to cause his mother distress.

With his hands fisted and heat boiling in his gut, he glanced at David and Peter. "Perhaps you had better stay close to town until next term starts. I may have need of you." Then he set off down the street, his stride long.

"Where are you off to?" David called out.

Wolviston threw his answer over his shoulder. "To see just how much trouble that devil has caused."

Twelve

He found his mother in her rooms. She came forward at once to greet him, her face troubled. "Oh, Evan, you would not credit what Lady Havers has just told me."

Cursing St. Albans for his meddling, Wolviston braced himself for the worst.

"Evan, it's horrible. Lord Byron is sailing from England the day after tomorrow."

Wolviston stared at her, unable to make sense of her words. Byron? Sailing? Then a laugh tickled inside him. His mother and Lady Havers had, it seemed, spoken about Lord Byron, whose marital problems had been mocked in the press and in scathing prints. Poor Byron had even been hissed at and booed in the streets by those who knew nothing more than that his lordship's wife had left him because of his bad ways. Had this been their terrible gossip?

He could almost laugh except he could not be certain, yet, that this was all she had heard. "Is he? I take it that Lady Havers came to call on you with this tattle?"

Lady Wolviston led him to a sofa. "She came to take tea at the hotel and we happened to meet. You must know that silly woman. She never forgets any face and so called to me at once, but she never has any fact entirely correct. She had the most nonsensical things to say about you being taken for some sort of rogue. I could not make sense of her sly hints.

"But when she told me of Byron, I had to get rid of her at once. Then I went to see Lady Melbourne, for she is a particular friend of Byron's. She confirmed that the sad news is indeed true. Oh, my dear, you know how I adored his cantos. I cannot help but think that he is being greatly wronged and that England is losing a truly great man."

"Yes, but he can write in other places, you know."

Lady Wolviston drew back. "You cannot possibly mean to suggest that anything he might write in some nasty foreign place will be half as good as if it were written here in England?"

Wolviston meant to suggest just that. However, he smiled and denied any such thing.

Byron's work, he knew, appealed to his mother for its romantic tragedy. That was, he presumed, also the appeal of the man's life. He was quite pleased to indulge her, and let her continue on about the misunderstood poet. Not only did it give her occupation—and a surprising amount of animation to her face and form—but it seemed a heaven-sent diversion from any rumors about him.

He stayed for a quarter hour and learned that Cousin Martha had indeed started the packing process. The news of Byron quitting Society had decided Lady Wolviston that she, too, would quit Society again. With luck, the ladies would be taking the family coach home that very day. Or at least he devoutly hoped so.

He took his leave of her, knowing that he would not feel entirely at ease until he heard she was safely back in the dower house at Wolviston Abbey. And, within a few days, the boys could start back for the next term at Cambridge.

That would leave him with one last problem—St. Albans.

He had to safeguard Clarissa from that trouble-making devil. And he could see only one path out of that dark maze.

Light from a hundred candles gave the ballroom a golden hue, and also an insufferable heat. A dozen perfumes mixed with the odor from those old-fashioned gentlemen who clung to the notion that bathing was unhealthy, and mingled with the reek of wine and the smells of roast meats from the supper room. Two hundred guests filled Lady Havers's house, crowding her ballroom, which had been hung with dozens of mirrors until it seemed a chamber of light and swirling color. Guests spilled into card rooms, for those who did not dance, and small salons for those seeking a place to sit down and talk about everyone else. The reception line had taken a good two hours to end. Just after midnight a beaming Lady Havers stood at the top of the stairs that led up to the third-floor ballroom.

The musicians sat at the far end of the rectangular room, their jumbled chords announcing the tuning of their instruments and that dancing would soon begin—if any room could be found.

Lady Havers turned her plump, smiling face to Clarissa, the ostrich feathers nodding in her elaborately curled hair. "What a sad crush. It is the success of the season, I think."

"Not everyone is here," Clarissa muttered, glancing around the crowded room in search of a familiar face.

She had greeted Lord St. Albans, who dressed all in black, other than his white shirt and cravat. He had seemed unusually pleased with himself, but Clarissa could do no more than welcome him and have her hand kissed. Then he had to move on and allow her to receive other guests.

Now, with her duty done to welcome those who came when they were bid, she could do as she pleased. Only she could not find the one man she wanted to see.

Where was Wolviston?

She had dressed with particular care. She wore yellow silk, so pale that it seemed almost white, and shot with the slightest of gold thread. Her maid had dressed her hair simply, winding a gold ribbon through the curls. Clarissa still wished that she had diamonds sparkling about her neck, but Lady Havers had declared jewels to be too sophisticated for Clarissa. Which was utter nonsense. Lady Havers herself wore enough diamonds and sapphires with her dark blue velvet to keep a jeweler in business a year.

Still, diamonds or no, Clarissa intended this evening to be a memorable one. She would flirt with every gentleman—except St. Albans and Wolviston. She would teach them that she would not tolerate their acting as if she were a prize to be won. However, it did no good to ignore only one of them, for he would simply feel that his rival was winning. She needed both of them here, so she could slight them equally.

Only where was Wolviston?

Irritation with him for not cooperating with her plans sparked and popped in her like sap on a fire. If he ruined her plans tonight, she would . . . well, she would do more than ignore him, although she did not know what that "more" was just yet.

She saw Reggie Preston and commandeered him into leading her out for the first dance, saying, "If you do not dance with me now, I shall make you dance twice with me later."

He went, glowering at her and complaining that he hated the minuet.

When that antiquated but traditional opening dance ended, the musicians struck up the first strains of a Scottish reel to let the guests know what the next dance would be. The musicians paused to allow the dancers to find partners, and Clarissa glanced at the gentlemen around her who clamored to have the honor of the next set.

Her court had thinned over the past few weeks, she noted, with a good deal of relief and only the slightest disappointment. Some gentlemen had stepped aside, reluctant to compete with St. Albans and Wolviston. And she saw that tonight Sir Anthony Lee had deserted her side for Jane's. *Well, at least someone is smiling,* she thought with a pang of envy for just how happy Jane looked. And then she chided herself. Jane of all people deserved happiness.

Turning, she smiled warmly at Lord Morrow. She

was just about to put her hand on his arm for him
to lead her out for the next dance when another
arm swept between them and a low voice said,
"Sorry, Morrow, old thing, but she promised me the
first country dance a week ago."

With a frown, she tried to tug her hand free from
Lord Wolviston's, but she could not even manage to
slip the fingertips of her gloves away from his firm
grip. He led her to the lines of dancers forming,
gentlemen on one side and ladies opposite.

"I did not promise you this dance," she said.

He kept hold of her hand and had the impudence
to smile. "And shall you now say that you do not
wish to dance with me?"

The music struck up. Ladies curtsied. Gentlemen
bowed. And Clarissa said, "I do not wish it."

The corner of Wolviston's mouth quirked. "That
makes us both liars."

She gave a huff, but the music had started and
the movement of the dance forced her to turn and
smile at the man next to Wolviston. At least, he
thought, with the strain easing from his shoulders,
she had not walked off the dance floor, leaving him
red-faced and solitary.

The movements of the dance pulled them apart
to dance with others and then put them together
again to walk through the steps. Bow, curtsy, turn
and twirl, step in place, two hands round, and then
again. The music swept on in a lively tempo, and
he had no time to do more than smile down at her,
and think that he ought not to tell her how beautiful
she looked. Some sort of pale fabric floated about
her, making her seem an ethereal creature. Of

course, the angry flashes in those huge blue eyes rather spoilt that effect.

"I meant to ignore you tonight," she said with a fixed smile when the dance next joined them.

His heart skipped a beat. They moved apart and he had to wait before he asked, "Why? Did St. Albans say something to you about me?"

She glanced up at him, a little puzzled. Then she had to turn to smile and dance with a corpulent fellow in a green coat and knee breeches. When she came back she said, "I do not care what he has to say about you, or what you have to say about him."

The dance separated them again and Wolviston swore under his breath. This was no place for conversation. He bit off his words and stepped through the dance until they had moved down to the end of the lines. Then he took Clarissa's hand and, opening a door behind them, slipped with her out of the ballroom.

"What are you? . . . Let go of me, my lord!"

He did not let go, but pulled her after him, his stride slowing a little to accommodate her smaller, dragging steps.

They were, he noted, in the supper room. Servants looked up from their tasks of laying out china and platters of food. The tart aroma of wine filled the room and Wolviston noticed that a river of the stuff ran like blood down the center of the main table.

"Charming notion," he muttered, still pulling Clarissa after him. He toyed with the notion of ordering the servants out, but it was not his house. Instead, he led Clarissa toward a set of French doors that let onto the back garden.

A moment later, he had her out on the stone terrace. Cool air, the earthly scent of dirt, and the spice of spring flowers wrapped around them. He would have run down the steps and into the garden, taking her with him, but she balked, pulling back on his hand with both of her own.

"I will not go another step with you. This is absurd. What do you think you are doing?"

Light from a full moon spilled onto her, turning her hair silver as fairy wings and her skin into glowing alabaster. Amid the dark shrubbery that lined the terrace, its colors and exact shape leached away by night's shadows, the narrow stone terrace seemed intimate and distant from the noise of the ballroom.

The night held enough chill to have discouraged others from venturing out. Thank heavens for small favors, thought Evan. Clarissa did not shiver, and he could only suspect that she was angry enough not to feel anything else.

"I wanted to talk to you," he said. "And I couldn't do it very well with you weaving in and out like that."

Clarissa glared at him. He looked sinfully handsome by moonlight. The pale light struck deep shadows from his strong profile. He loomed before her, tall and formidable, and the anticipation of what he might do fluttered in her stomach. She rather liked the sensation, but she held onto her irritation as if it were her armor.

Turning aside, she walked to the balustrade and settled her gloved hands on the stone railing. "Very well. Talk to me, if you must."

He said nothing, but she heard the scuff of his evening shoes on the stone and his heat washed over her back as he came closer. The flutter in her stomach fell lower. She glanced at him over her shoulder and wet her lips. Would he kiss her?

Taking her shoulders, he turned her to face him. He had stripped off his gloves and his fingers seemed to burn through the thin silk of her gown.

Wolviston frowned at her. She was not making this easy. And she, the little devil, knew it. She stood there before him, that willful chin lifted, her eyes sparkling brighter than the stars, and that luscious mouth set in a pout. She ought to be nervous with him. Hell, she ought not to be here with him. But, it seemed, she would never learn that lesson. No, she thought she could handle anything. Himself. St. Albans. Anything. Naivete and determination were her strengths, and her great weaknesses.

Lord, he ought not to do this. Only, what other choice did he have? He could not step aside and leave her, so trusting and inviting, for St. Albans to ruin. He had made himself responsible by starting this deception, and so he would see it to its finish. And some-day—some long, distant day from now, he prayed—he would tell her the truth, and they would laugh about it. Oh, God, he hoped they would laugh.

Taking her hand, he went down on one knee. Her lips parted with surprise. She caught her breath and one hand fluttered up the sweet curve of her breast.

He swallowed to empty the dryness from his mouth, and then he said, "Clarissa, you must know that when I met you my life changed." *And that's true enough.* He went on, trying to think what other nonsense he ought to mutter to make it sound right. "I have tried to ignore what I felt, but I cannot. I am not a perfect man—" *Lord, was he ever not, but not in the ways she thought him flawed.* "—but if you do me the honor of becoming my wife, I vow to be better. I will do all I can to make you the happiest of women."

Clarissa's breath lay trapped in her chest, lodged there until it ached to break free. She could only stare down at him, her gaze fixed and unblinking. She had expected him to steal a kiss perhaps, but not this. She gulped down a ragged breath. A smile trembled on her lips and inside her chest. Did he mean it?

Her head spun as if she had drunk too much. "You . . . you catch me by surprise."

He rose to his feet. "Evan. My name is Evan."

"Evan," she repeated, as if mesmerized.

Stripping off her right glove, he raised her hand to his lips. The edge of his jaw, freshly shaved, brushed across the back of her hand and she marveled at the tingle that raced up her arm to her chest. Leaning closer to him, the scent of him, spicy and warm, teased at her.

"Evan, I don't know what to say," she told him, startled into honesty. She stared into his shadowed eyes and wished she could better see if those gray eyes had darkened with desire, or if they were troubled, or alight with some other emotion.

He pressed her hand to his lips. "Tell me I have the right to protect you, to call you my lady. Tell me that and I swear I will give up this empty life I have been leading here in London. I vow that I'll be a husband who never gives you a moment's worry. There will be no other woman, save for you. I shall give up gaming, I shall give up anything you ask, if you will but say yes."

Smiling up at him, the word trembled on her lips. But one small, nagging doubt held her still. He had said so much, but he had not said the word *love* even once. Confusion swirled in her. Her chest tightened, as did her grip on his hand.

"I . . . I . . ." she said, stumbling over the words.

His breath warmed her face as he leaned over her, and then his lips brushed across hers. For an instant, joy fluttered inside her.

And then he pulled back.

She stared up at him, blinking. What was that? A kiss? A gentleman's respectful, brief kiss?

Disappointment flooded her. Her face twisted with it.

He was acting just like a gentleman. Gone indeed was the man who had kissed her silly in her godmother's conservatory and who had then walked away. Gone, too, was the passion in that wicked kiss.

He had reformed, it seemed. And she wanted to cry for what she had once tasted and had now lost.

Tears tickled the back of her nose and stung her eyes. *I don't want you like this,* she wanted to tell him. Her fists clenched on his chest. She struck at him with both of them and let out an anguished, muffled sob.

"What is it? What's wrong? What have I done?" he demanded.

A man's voice, clipped and harsh, answered from the open doorway behind them. "Excellent questions. And I hope that one of you has some excellent answers for me."

Clarissa twisted away from Wolviston. Shock washed cold and tingling over her face and hands. She stared at the dark figure in the doorway and said, her voice barely audible, "Uncle Andrew?"

Thirteen

Dressed in dusty riding clothes and looking travel weary, Lord Rothe loomed in the doorway. "The question is, Miss, what are you doing out here, alone with this fellow?"

Clarissa put a hand up to rub her temple. "Oh, this is like some bad dream!"

Evan glanced at her, frowning and worried. She had paled even more, if that were possible, and he could see the pulse fluttering too rapidly at the base of her throat. Uncle or no, the fellow had no right to overset her in this fashion.

"You pick the devil of a way to bid your niece hello," he said, glaring at the man he presumed must be Andrew Derhurst, Lord Rothe, Clarissa's guardian and uncle.

A dark-eyed stare fixed on Wolviston with unnerving intensity. "And you, sir, pick the devil of a place to make love to my niece. Are you Wolviston or St. Albans?"

"Evan Fortesque, Lord Wolviston," Evan said with a curt bow. "And I've . . ."

"No, do not start to explain now. This is no place for privacy, and you should remember that the next time you do not wish an interruption. Come with me."

Lord Rothe stepped back and held open the door, his mouth set in a taut line and one dark eyebrow cocked. He was a tall man with a military stiffness to his shoulders. Gray feathered his dark hair, making him look damnably formidable, Evan thought, as he shepherded Clarissa back into the house.

Ignoring the speculative stares of the servants, Rothe summoned a footman with no more than a lift of his hand. He commanded a private room, and was bowed into the small study at the back of the house. Once there, he turned to the wide-eyed footman and ordered two brandies. Then he glanced at Clarissa and changed his order to three glasses of wine.

Clarissa sat, her face averted from her uncle, her lips pressed tightly together as if she were struggling to maintain a dignified poise. Color had returned to her cheeks. One elbow-length glove was in place, but she had lost the other one. Her eyes glittered, bright as snow-fed lakes. Evan took that as a bad sign. Why the devil did the uncle have to show up now, of all times?

Rothe positioned himself in front of the unlit fireplace, his hands clasped behind his back. Once drinks were brought and the servants had left, he turned to Clarissa. "Now, Miss. Explain yourself."

"And what have I to explain, Uncle?" she said, her voice quivering with indignation. "I did not burst in on you."

Lord Rothe smiled. "And you are not my guardian, either. So you will explain what the devil you have been up to. I should never have allowed Maeve to talk me into sending you to London with no better a keeper than your godmother."

"I do not require a keeper."

"You, Miss, require a lock and key!"

Evan set down his wineglass and stepped forward before the tension in the room exploded. "Lord Rothe, I ought to have applied to you first, but I will do so now and tell you that I have just asked Clarissa to be my wife."

Black eyes fixed on him and Evan could almost wish he had kept quiet. "It matters not when you ask me, sir, for my answer is the same. My niece is in my care until she is twenty-five. And she is not marrying any damn rake."

"Uncle!" Clarissa said, jumping to her feet. "How dare you say such things to him? You are being rude—and unfair!"

"Do not try me, my girl. I have had a long trip and am not inclined to indulge you just now. Your letters home have had your aunt worrying and your mother fretting over you."

"It is my life to lead."

"And it is those who love you most who would suffer if you ruin yourself. Which means that I shall not allow you to ally yourself with a man who would make you—and therefore your aunt and mother—miserable."

"I will marry as I choose! And I will not stand here and let you insult Evan—I mean, Lord Wolviston. He has acted as a true gentleman to me."

"A gentleman who kisses you on a dark terrace?" Rothe said, his voice dry.

The color flared brighter on Clarissa's cheeks. "With honorable intentions, sir!"

Lord Rothe lifted one dark eyebrow. Then he turned his stare on Wolviston. "Honorable, is it? Sir, the reputation I have heard mentioned tonight by Lady Havers, and on other occasions by my niece's very pen, is not a good one. You are known to gamble to excess, to womanize, and in general to raise more hell than is good for you. Or have I got that all wrong somehow?"

Clarissa stamped her foot. "Uncle!"

Heat and anger swelled in Evan at Lord Rothe's curt words, which cut into him like a whip on his skin. However, he put a restraining hand out to Clarissa and met Lord Rothe's implacable judgment with his own temper on a tight leash. "I could lie, sir, but I have the feeling you know the truth when you hear it."

"I do, sir. And I will."

Evan straightened and kept his stare locked on Rothe's. He knew the danger of what he was doing. But he was damned either way just now. And he could not—would not—be the cause of an estrangement between Clarissa and her family.

He glanced once more at Clarissa, trying to will her to understand, and then he turned back to Lord Rothe. "I will not lie to you, my lord. I am a fraud, but I am no rake."

Feeling Clarissa's stare on him, Evan glanced at her, half afraid what he would see. Slowly, she sank down on her chair, for once out of words. Confusion clouded her gaze, and pain lay dark in the center of those wide blue eyes. Evan's throat tightened as if he had just put a noose around his neck, and he looked away, detesting himself for ever having thought of this game.

"And how is it that all of London, myself and my niece included, thinks you a rake?" Rothe asked, his black eyebrows arched over his dark eyes.

Evan wanted to pull at his too-tight cravat, but he merely flexed his fingers and then began an explanation.

He did not look at Clarissa as he spoke, but kept his gaze on Lord Rothe, trying to judge from the man's hard expression what he might be thinking. The gilt clock on the mantel chimed the half-hour, and the distant sound of music carried from the ballroom as if it came from some other reality. Clarissa's perfume still lay in his nostrils, and dug more guilt into him as he remembered the taste of her lips and the soft sigh of her breath on his.

He started with the very beginning, with seeing Clarissa in the garden and overhearing her dismissal of boring gentlemen. Clarissa pulled in a sharp breath at that, but Evan kept talking.

Lord Rothe's expression never changed. However, as Evan hanged himself further with his tale, he thought he caught the faintest glimmer of humor in the man's black eyes. Or perhaps it was a glimmer of something far more dangerous, he thought, uneasy.

Finally, when he had run out of words, he glanced at Clarissa. She sat with her face lowered, so that he could only see her golden curls. He ached to tuck his fingers under that stubborn chin and lift her face so that he could see into her eyes and know what she was feeling.

But she had shut him out of the intimacy of her thoughts.

He glanced back at Lord Rothe.

His lordship studied his empty wineglass for a moment, then asked, "So you posed as a rake to teach my niece a lesson? You are, in fact, an honorable gentleman?"

Evan winced at the sarcasm, but he knew he deserved it. "The story does me no credit, but my reputation as a rogue is highly exaggerated—by myself." He glanced at Clarissa. "And once I had started, my lord, I found that I did not wish to lose your niece's regard."

At that, Clarissa had to look up. A storm raged inside her, so fierce that she could not trust herself to say anything. Her fingers had numbed from clasping them too tight. He had not meant any of it—not the kiss in the conservatory, not the looks he had given her, not the things he had told her. Misery twisted inside her. He thought her a fool. A little idiot who needed a lesson on life.

She looked down and blinked hard. Not for anything would she let him see that he could make her cry. Not even tears of anger.

"So you're only a minor rogue?" her uncle said, a touch of humor in his voice which made her cringe. They were both laughing at her dreams. At her. They thought her a child to be humored. Then her uncle made it worse by adding, "You may not know this, sir, but you appeared quite often in Clarissa's letters home. A recent lack of mentions left my wife reading between the lines, and thinking you would break Clarissa's heart. My wife had . . . rather personal experiences with a rogue who did not mean anything honorable, you see."

Clarissa looked up, unable to keep quiet. "This is nothing like what . . ."

"Hush, Clarissa. I will deal with you in a moment."

Taking her upper lip between her teeth, Clarissa gripped her hands together again and turned away.

Lord Rothe went on. "Well, Wolviston, I cannot applaud this little diversion of yours, but it is, I must say, certainly worthy of one of Clarissa's schemes."

She sat up, outraged. It did not seem to matter that Wolviston's masquerade had been at her expense. He was a gentleman, after all. He could be forgiven his little fun. And was she now supposed to do all the forgiving?

"I still mean to ask further about you, Wolviston, but if you are not the devil we thought, then I withdraw my objection. Clarissa, since the fellow's kissed you already, it looks as if you have a husband-to-be."

That did it. Now, she was to marry him. She was to smile and not worry about such unnecessary details as love. Oh, she hated them both. Hated them. Hated! Her hand itched to slap Wolviston's face. She wanted to scream and throw things at her horrible uncle. But she would show them, instead, that she was no longer such a child.

Burying her pain under a hot layer of anger, she buried that, in turn, under an icy, smiling façade. Two could play this game of pretend. She glanced once at her uncle, and then rose to face Wolviston.

He eyed her, wary.

You have good cause to worry, you snake! she thought, smiling even more. Then she said, "Oh, lud, Uncle. I have never had any intent to marry Lord Wolviston." She forced a small laugh. "You see, I already knew of his deception. I only wanted to see how far he would go with it."

Doubt shadowed Wolviston's gray eyes. "You knew?"

She gave a small shrug. "I guessed a short time ago—just before I stopped writing home about you, in fact. Of course, I did not know, or care, really, why you invented this pretense. How sweet that you kept it up for no better reason than that you wanted to keep my fond regard."

He had the courtesy to flinch. "Clarissa, you cannot know how sorry I am if any of this has caused you the least distress."

"Distress?" She forced another brittle laugh. She wished her uncle had shot Wolviston when he had first come upon them. She wished she could shoot him now herself. But she only smiled at him and said, "Distress. La, sir, as if you could. My affections were never the least engaged."

Lord Rothe's voice cut in, sharp and cold as a North Sea wind. "Do you mean to say you've been allowing men to kiss you with no intention of marriage?"

She shot a glance at him over her shoulder. The tremor inside her had grown and she did not know how much longer she could hold her pose. But she would die before she let either of them see anything but a sophisticated lady who knew better than they how to play these games.

"Yes, it is all my fault, is it not? It is my fault Lord Wolviston put on wolf's clothes, when he is in fact a sheep. . . ."

"A what?" Wolviston said, starting to frown.

Ignoring him, she went on. "It is my fault that men act like idiots around me. It is always my fault, and I shall no doubt end up badly, but I shall tell you this, Uncle! I shall end up with real passion in my life!'' She turned and looked Wolviston up and down. "I have acquired a strong distaste for poor imitations."

Anger tightened Wolviston's mouth and the shadows in his eyes deepened. Elation rose in her that she had been able to wound him. But dismay tainted her victory. Why did he have to look at her that way, as if she were some heartless creature he did not know?

"You shall have to pardon me," she said, her voice catching in her throat. "I promised the next dance to Lord St. Albans."

The room started to blur as she strode for the door. She had to get out. Now. Before the maelstrom inside her burst free. Her shaking hand clasped the door knob and she fumbled with it, then she had it open. She wanted to slam it with all her strength, but she forced herself to shut it behind her with a soft click.

Then she glared at the dark oak. A sob caught in her throat. She pulled in a deep breath and pressed her hand to her chest.

No, she would not cry over him. She had not. She would not.

Respectable gentlemen, she thought with utter scorn. She was through with them forever.

Turning on her heel, she started for the ballroom, intent on proving to herself just how little she cared for the man she had left behind.

Evan glanced at Lord Rothe. "That did not go well, did it?"

Lord Rothe moved to the decanter that had been

brought in earlier. He filled his glass and Wolviston's, then said, "On the contrary. She did not shatter every breakable in the room over your back. Maeve was right. London Society has done her some good."

Picking up his wine, Evan swirled the red liquid. The smell of oak and grape wound around him like a sensual presence, reminding him again of Clarissa. "But I have not." He set his glass down. "I'll leave at once."

Lord Rothe put a hand on his arm. "I have seen enough foolish pride for the night. Sit down, drink your wine, and tell me just why you started this lark. And do not say it was because of my niece's scorn. That might have been the spark, but there was a fuse for her to light and set you off as she did."

"Lord Rothe, I . . ."

"And you may call me Andrew, or Rothe, or sir. But if you keep 'lording' me, I shall be the one who breaks the knick-knackery across your skull."

Rothe offered a rare smile, and Evan found himself smiling back. He took up his wine and sat down, and found himself starting to talk about things he had no intention of talking about—his father's accident, his brothers' troubles, his mother's smothering worries. It came out slowly, with Rothe asking terse questions. Evan talked and drank, and Lord Rothe listened with a flattering attention that made Wolviston realize how much he had missed having an older man of sense to speak with.

Four glasses of wine later, the clock on the mantel chimed two and Wolviston sat up with a guilty start. "I'm prosing on like an old man on his deathbed."

Rothe smiled. "It's shock. That and the wine. But

I should get to know the man who plans to marry my brother's only daughter."

Evan's mouth twisted. "That will not be me."

"Oh? Why did you ask her to marry you then?"

"Truth is, I could see no other option. I thought I had built expectations in her. I was responsible for that, and for starting this game. So I wanted to end it with as little hurt to her as I could manage."

"Expectations? You are on a path to hell if you think you can fulfill those for her." He leaned forward so that his elbows rested on his knees. "My niece is spoilt, impulsive, willful, and has a head full of romantic nonsense from too many years spent in her own fantasies. I blame her mother for not correcting those faults. But Clarissa is also generous, has a kind heart, is more sensitive than you would credit, and she is in grave need of a match with someone who can encourage the best in her without giving in to the worst. In short, she needs a man who can love her enough to tell her when she is being an idiot."

Evan gave a rueful smile. "That's a difficult thing to tell a beautiful woman."

"Not if you love the woman more than you love the beauty. And that is the problem. It is damn hard for any man to get past those curves of hers and those charms she wields. She's a lethal minx. But you should know that after seeing her performance tonight."

"Her performance was no worse than my own. And I deserved it."

"You did. And you shall get even more dramatic encores if you're still intent on wedding her. However, you have done the honorable thing and offered for her. It is no dishonor to leave it at that and leave her to whatever nonsense she is set on now."

Evan put down his wineglass and stood. "Thank you, sir."

He knew that Rothe was right. He should go. He had done all he could. So why was he not happy? The truth was out and he would not have to marry.

But his stomach twisted at the thought that now she would never forgive him. He could not possibly care about that, yet he did. And the fear lay cold on his skin that perhaps he had been a fool after all.

He could not forget the pain in her eyes. And he could not stop wishing he could undo the past.

And he could not see how she would ever believe him if he told her that he had only just realized that he loved her.

Stupid, stupid girl. So easily fooled. Turning her face up to her partner, Clarissa smiled even wider, and laughed as if she had never enjoyed any man's company as much.

The dance ended, and another began. She bestowed her favors without discrimination. She flirted with the gentlemen until even Jane whispered a word of warning to her, and then she turned on Jane and told her not to be such an utter stick about life. The shock on Jane's face twisted the wretchedness inside Clarissa into something even worse. She turned away from her friend, ashamed but unable to admit it.

She danced every dance. She drank anything put in her hand. She laughed and said any shocking thing that came to mind. Some of the gentlemen tried to get her to sit down, but others encouraged her with their laughter and increasingly bawdy language.

The only taste of pleasure she had was to see Sir Anthony Lee turn to console an unhappy-looking Jane. But the glow on Jane's face as she put her hand into Sir Anthony's for the quadrille, and the smile he gave her, almost unwound Clarissa's control. She turned away at once, before she burst into tears.

At dawn, the musicians stopped playing. Clarissa wanted to demand that they go on, but Lady Havers was already bidding the last guests good night.

The distractions were all leaving and Clarissa turned to Lord St. Albans, desperate not to be left with her own thoughts.

Grasping his hand, she begged him to stay.

"What is this? You have not been so fond of me before."

She laughed and took his hands and spun him around once. Then she stopped and stared at him hard. "Have you ever lied to me?"

He tilted his head. "Do you want me to lie to you?"

"No. I never want lies. Do you love me?"

He leaned close and his expression turned suddenly intense, as if only the two of them existed in the world. "I want you as I have never wanted any woman."

A small thrill chased through her, but so did a queasy uncertainty. She looked up at St. Albans, at his dangerous, sharp features. "I cannot trust you, can I?"

He smiled again.

She bit her lower lip. He had said he wanted her, but had not said a word about love or marriage. Was Lady Havers right, after all? With a rake, did the love perhaps come afterwards? Even her namesake in Mr. Richardson's novel, even that Clarissa, had found love only after her ruination.

St. Albans took her ungloved hand in his. She had danced all night wearing only one glove. Ladies had talked, and two of the more dashing girls had copied her and stripped off a single glove as well.

"I am not a man to trust," St. Albans said. "But that's not what you want, is it?" He kissed her hand, and then turned it over and kissed the inside of her wrist, his lips brushing across where her pulse fluttered.

"Just send me word, my sweet mystery, and I shall not only help you learn all that you desire, but I will give it to you as well." He stared into her eyes for a long moment, then he bowed and left her.

She watched him leave then, her heart heavy, but still putting on smiles and chattering nonsense, she at last had no place to go but to her room. And after her maid had dressed her for bed, the silence settled around her, leaving her no escape from her thoughts.

What was she going to do tomorrow? She would have to see Lord Wolviston again sometime. Would he spread the story of how he had fooled her? She had almost told others tonight, to make him sound ridiculous, but she had not been able to do it. She hated him. But she could not spread a story that would leave him laughed at, scorned like poor Lord Byron had been.

What if he did come to see her? What if she weakened? What if her uncle insisted that she marry him?

"I won't marry him. I don't love him," she muttered. And she did not. She loved something that did not exist. "Fool, fool, fool," she muttered, pacing the room with each word.

But what if he kept coming to see her? What if he kept asking her to marry him?

Oh, she could not stay. She did not trust her hate to remain strong, and if she weakened, she would make them both miserable forever. He might deserve it, but she wanted better.

Tugging on the bell-rope, she rang for her maid, and then began to give orders to pack.

By ten the next morning she sat on her bed, exhausted. Her bags sat stacked by the window, her clothes packed away, and her maid, almost as bedraggled as Clarissa felt, eyed her warily. Clarissa didn't care. She didn't care about any of it.

She would go home.

She would forget about him.

"I shall just rest for a bit," she said, lying down on her bed, still in her dressing gown. Clarissa lay on her side, and heard the maid quietly shut the door.

Pressing the back of her hand to her mouth, she turned her face into the bedding and let exhaustion overcome her.

"I shall take her home tomorrow," Lord Rothe said.

Lady Havers looked up from her breakfast and blinked. "You shall what? Take her home? And how in the world is Lord Wolviston ever to mend things between them if you drag her off to the wilds of Yorkshire? Oh, yes, that would be a very nice thing to do just now."

Rothe frowned and drummed his fingers on the breakfast table. "What do you know of Wolviston and my niece?"

With a sigh, Lady Havers put down her silver and faced his lordship. She had been delighted to see him last night—a handsome man was always welcome in her house. But she should have known he would be trouble. Men with such uncompromising chins always were trouble.

"You may think me a goose, and I know you do, so do not deny it. And I am just a little. But I should have to be an utter noddy not to notice the glow on her face when she looks at him, or not to see how he cannot stay away from her. That is what I know."

"Then you ought to also know that my niece damn near made a scandal of herself last night! I saw how she behaved."

"And what else was she to do? Meekly cry her heart out because of a disagreement? If you think that, you do not know your own niece!"

"Oh, I know her. Which is why I am loath to leave her in London," Rothe said, scowling.

Picking up her silver again, Lady Havers addressed her buttered toast and eggs. "Well, if you do not, those two will certainly never make a match of it. Your time would be better spent trying to keep Wolviston here as well."

The door to the breakfast room opened and Clarissa came in, pale-faced and quiet, wearing a blue wool traveling dress. Lady Havers took in the

girl's blank stare with more alarm than she cared to
show. Her Ladyship knew that matters between dear
Clarissa and Lord Wolviston hung in a delicate balance. She did not know all the details, but she certainly knew the signs of love gone very wrong.

"My dear, going out for a drive?" Lady Havers
asked with a smile.

Clarissa sat down at the round table. "I want to
go home."

Lady Havers shot an alarmed glance at Lord
Rothe and then held her breath. It all rested with
him now.

Rothe glanced from his niece to Lady Havers,
then picked up his newspaper and rose. "You
wanted a season in London, Miss. So you will stay
the season out."

Lady Havers released her breath and started to
smile, and then Lord Rothe ruined it all by adding,
"And if Wolviston calls, you are to see him and treat
him kindly. The man's a decent fellow and better
than you deserve."

Clarissa pushed back her chair and stood up to
glare at her uncle. "Perhaps you can dictate where
I may go, but you cannot force me to receive a man
I find loathsome."

Wishing she could kick him, Lady Havers rose, too,
and came around to take Clarissa's hand. "Oh, I am
certain your uncle did not mean you must see him."

"Yes he does," Clarissa said, her voice tight. Then
she turned away and fled.

Fourteen

In her room, Clarissa turned the key and locked herself in. She paced the room, her nerves frayed by fatigue and wretchedness. She knew what would happen. They would wear her down—her uncle and Wolviston. They would keep at her and at her and eventually she would have to see him again, and . . . oh, but she did not trust herself. She would be weak. She would forgive him. He would trick her again with lies that she wanted to believe, and then they would spend the rest of their lives in quiet misery—a gentleman and the wife he did not love. And she would grow vain and he would grow bitter. And he would one day hate her.

She bit her knuckle.

He did not love her. He had never said that he did. The best she could hope for would be for him to give her a polite lie and say that he did. And she could not bear being married to a man who thought her a beautiful idiot.

She could not bear it.

So she went instead to her desk and dipped her quill into the inkwell and began to write a note to Lord St. Albans.

* * *

"You look like the very devil," Reggie said, striding into The Rose. He sprawled onto a chair and eyed his friend. A day's worth of beard shadowed Wolviston's jaw. His eyes glittered from drink and his dark clothes and black cravat made him look the most dangerous man in the room. No wonder he sat alone, with the tables nearby left empty.

Wolviston lifted his drink in a mocking toast. "To devils, and to the hell we make for ourselves with the lies we tell. Have you come to collect on our bet?"

Reggie held up a hand to the tavern wench to order an ale, and then turned back to his friend. "They weren't lies, exactly. And I told half of 'em. And you ought to look on the bright side. You may have lost a bet, but at least you don't have to be worried about being tied down with a wife just yet."

Wolviston lifted his head, such a bleak look in his eyes that Reggie wished he had not said anything. Oh, damn, but he knew what he was like. He fell in love, it seemed, every other month. The falling-in part was easy. It was the other side of it that turned a fellow inside-out.

"What I meant to say," Reggie said, blustering on, hoping to find something to cheer his friend, "is that you don't have to marry the Derhurst chit to keep her safe from St. Albans. Though, I daresay, you haven't really had to worry about that since her uncle appeared in town."

"Reggie, what are you bleating on about?"

"The gossip. What? Haven't you heard? St. Albans has a new ladybird. Hadlington even saw his carriage on the north road with a little beauty tucked inside. And I heard that St. Albans was overheard talking to the Prince Regent and saying that he was even thinking of going abroad with his latest charmer. That is, if she still interests him after a fortnight."

Evan had grown quiet as Reggie spoke, and now Reggie eyed his friend, deeply ill at ease.

Over the past three days since Lady Havers's ball the man had taken to gaming rashly and drinking deeply. Word had spread that Wolviston's reputation was a sham, but no one believed that rumor. Not when the man had become almost a regular at the most disreputable dens of iniquity. He wasn't a rake yet, Reggie thought, but he'd never seen a man so bent on becoming one in rapid order.

Damn that Derhurst girl.

Smiling, trying to rally his friend, Reggie leaned forward. "What say we go early to Brighton, eh? Your brothers are back at school, and the season will sputter on for a month or more, but there's . . ."

"Is she blonde?"

"Beg pardon?"

Evan fixed a drink-bright stare on Reggie. "St. Albans's new charmer? Is she blonde?"

"Devil if I know. What do you—? Oh, no. No. You cannot be thinking that. Even St. Albans would not dare to carry off a respectable girl from under her uncle's nose. She's Lord Rothe's niece, not some nobody's daughter."

Evan stared into his brandy. Reggie was right. Even St. Albans would hesitate to run away with a nobleman's niece. Or would he? Would he think beyond anything but those wide blue eyes, those sweet curves, those pouting lips? His own pulse fired as he thought of her in St. Albans's arms. The image rose of her and St. Albans at the masquerade, and he tormented himself further with picturing her turning a laughing face toward that devil.

Truth was, St. Albans would dare anything.

So would Clarissa.

Cursing under his breath, Evan rose to his feet, his chair scraping on the rough planked floor.

Reggie's glass paused in midair as he glanced up, a startled look on his face. "Are we leaving?"

Tossing a half-crown on the table, Evan strode to the door. "Stay if you like. I have a call to pay."

"What? Now? Evan . . . Evan! Oh, dash it all, wait up, will you?"

Night had settled over London by the time Evan raised the brass knocker on Lady Havers's door. Reggie stood beside him, shifting from foot to foot, glancing back at the hired hack that had taken them to Berkley Square and muttering predictions against Evan's suspicions.

Evan had to pound twice before Bentley appeared with the news that her ladyship was out, and Lord Rothe had gone to dine at The Guards, a club for military men.

"Where's Clar—is Miss Derhurst at home?" Evan demanded.

Lady Havers's butler eyed the gentleman, and then seemed to decide that divulging such information might be the only way to clear them from the doorstep. "She left with her ladyship for Vauxhall, my lord."

Stuffing his hands in his breeches pockets, Evan grumbled a thanks and turned away from the house, restless and still troubled.

"Satisfied?" Reggie said, sounding relieved. "The

chit is out enjoying herself, while you're eating your heart out."

Evan glanced back at the darkened house. "Is she?"

Frowning, Reggie pleaded, "Evan, please tell me you aren't thinking of trying to track down Rothe with these mad suspicions?"

"No. If I were certain . . ." He trailed off, staring at the pale stone front of Lady Havers's town house. Damn, but he could not make more trouble between Clarissa and her uncle. But there was another way to settle his fears. A glimmer of devilment danced inside him, half of it due to drink and half of it to a damn dangerous mood. He turned to Reggie and clapped a hand on his friend's shoulder. "However, there's another place where I don't mind making myself unwelcome."

Reggie gripped his friend's arm. "No, Evan. You cannot be thinking of that. You don't even know where St. Albans might be."

"If he's taken the road north, I have a damn good guess that it's not for Gretna Green. But the town of St. Albans lies not twenty miles north of us, and does he not have a house there? A house that everyone knows he uses for his ladybirds?"

Reggie fixed a stern look on his friend. "Evan, the Earl of St. Albans is a friend of the Prince, a crack shot, and, by all that's reckoned, a damn dangerous fellow."

Shaking off Reggie's grip, Evan started for the hired carriage. "Ah, but so am I, Reggie. So am I now."

"More wine?" St. Albans asked, already pouring the golden liquid into Clarissa's goblet.

She smiled at him, then lifted the cool crystal to her lips. The wine smelled of spice and summer warmth and trickled down her throat like honey. She drank it back and held up her glass for more.

After over an hour's rattling drive in a carriage that had swayed so hard from the galloping horses that she had had to clutch the leather straps to stay upright, it had been a relief to arrive at Holywell House. A small brick building, covered in ivy, it lay nestled in a clearing, not far from the tiny village they had driven through. She had no clear recollection of the village, other than it seemed to have no more than three or four houses which she had only glimpsed. But she liked this house, with its cozy rooms and its tasteful decorations. It did not look like a den of seduction and ruination.

Her mouth dried and she drank more wine, hoping it would make this adventure seem more like an adventure and less like a horrible mistake. St. Albans had, after all, promised her that he adored her. And perhaps by morning she would adore him as well. She desperately hoped so.

Rising from the table, he pulled back her chair and took her hand, his touch cool and light. He led her from the dining room to a parlor where a fire burned.

The flames danced on the patterned carpet and made shadows leap across the blue silk hung on the walls. Small, intimate, the room held a sofa which faced the fireplace, a round table with a decanter, two chairs, and a half-moon table that stood against the wall. There, three candles burned in a silver candelabra and fragrant yellow roses stood in a crystal vase.

He moved closer to her and she moved away, saying, "Do you know, I have not seen a single servant since we arrived."

"They are trained to be invisible."

"I heard of a duke who does that," she said, stepping to the mantel to admire a porcelain figure of a hunter and his dog. "His staff even has to turn their faces to the walls when he walks by. Must your staff do that?"

He took the porcelain from her hand and set it back on the mantel. "I do not want to talk about servants when I have your beauty to adore."

"Oh," she said, and looked away.

"Clarissa, what am I to say? How am I to make love to you? Most women cannot hear enough of such sweet words as I could give you, and yet you do not want any of them."

Moving away from him, she paused to finger a tapestry that hung opposite the long, curtained windows. "If I were most women, I do not think I would be here with you, now would I?"

He gave a small laugh and came to her. "No, you would not."

He took her by her shoulders and his eyes darkened. Her pulse jumped. She wanted to pull away again, but his hands tightened, keeping her still. She knew that the moment had come. She could not put it off. Well, she had come to him, knowing this would happen, expecting it, wanting it. She squeezed her eyes shut, lifted her face, and waited, her breath tight in her chest.

His lips touched hers—warm, questing, not unpleasant—and then he pulled away. She opened her eyes a little to find him staring down at her, his mouth thinned and his eyes hard. An instant later, he was smiling at her again.

Keeping his hand on her arm, he led her to the sofa. "Let's try this sitting down, shall we?"

She came unresisting, but without any eagerness, and St. Albans had to control the desire to shake her. He could move her arms, place her in position, and she allowed it all without participation. Devil a bit, but he could buy a better dolly in any alley in London.

Seating her on one end of the sofa, he lounged opposite her. She looked desirable. Firelight glimmered in that golden hair. Her white muslin dress clung to her curves in tantalizing ways. Her mouth turned down in a slight pout. So why did such a picture inspire a growing boredom?

Damn the girl.

This was to have been a lovely moment. She had summoned him, had she not? She had been the one to say yes to his proposition, which had left out any mention of marriage. She had shown him that he had been right to believe that there really was, in this wicked world, no such thing as true innocence. So why was her blasted willingness so irritating?

Damn the girl.

St. Albans rose. He did not pace. He hated men who paced, for it revealed an indecisive personality. Instead, he went to the brandy decanter and poured himself a drink—and one for her as well.

Then he came back. What was wrong with her?

She could not be in love with that impostor. She had spent the entire journey from London talking of Wolviston. Of his deception. Of his perfidy. He had let her, thinking she would get it out of her system. And he had enjoyed watching the anger flash in her eyes.

But where was that fire now?

Damn the girl. What did he have to do, drag out Wolviston's name every five minutes?

A clattering of hooves and carriage wheels outside interrupted. St. Albans glanced up, and Clarissa, startled, spilled her drink on the carpet. She rose and turned, clutching her brandy glass. St. Albans also rose.

An instant later a dark figure in a greatcoat burst into the room, throwing open the door. The man tossed his hat onto a chair and stepped toward the firelight, and St. Albans relaxed. Well, perhaps this would spark some life back into the girl. And he didn't mind having the chance to be rid of the damn fellow in a more permanent fashion.

"Hallo, Wolviston," he drawled. "Is it pistols now, or do you want a drink first?"

Evan glanced at St. Albans, then his stare riveted on Clarissa. He had not seen her in the past three days. His heart gave a hard lurch at the sight of her, and the ache inside him settled deeper into his bones. Her face looked thinner—or was it that her eyes seemed larger? He frowned and searched her for signs of harm; then his shoulders eased down as he saw the light spark in her eyes and that stubborn chin rise.

She folded her hands in front of her. "Good evening, Lord Wolviston. Did my uncle send you, or are you on your own fool's errand?"

Wolviston eased out of his greatcoat and threw it on the chair that held his hat. Then he turned to St. Albans. "You mentioned pistols?"

"And a drink. There's brandy in the decanter."

Evan started for the inlaid round table that held a

crystal decanter and three goblets. "I'll take the drink. It's too dark just now for dueling and it's starting to rain."

Clarissa glared at him. "You are already drunk!"

"No, I'm half drunk. Besides, I thought excess endeared a man to you." He glanced at St. Albans. "That and telling you what you want to hear, that is."

St. Albans arched one eyebrow. "Careful. Or you may have to face pistols, whether you will or no."

Wolviston shot him a reckless grin.

Thunking her glass down on the mantel, Clarissa turned to Wolviston. "You are drunk! And you are . . ."

"A hateful liar, I know. And I tricked you and I'm the very devil of a fellow. That's usually the sort of fellow you most admire, but not in my case, I take it?"

She gave a low growl, and he let an unrepentant smile twist up the corner of his mouth. A porcelain figure sailed past his head and shattered on the wall. He glanced at it, then at Clarissa, and turned to St. Albans. "I'll pay for the china."

St. Albans turned from admiring the fire that had flared to life in Clarissa. It irritated him enormously that Wolviston had been the one to reanimate her, and it left him a nasty dilemma. If he threw Wolviston out, or shot the fellow, then out went Clarissa's fire. But he could not very well seduce her under the man's territorial stare.

Folding his arms, St. Albans gave a shrug and waited to see what would develop. "The china is no matter. A gift from an aunt, and a rather ugly one at that. Both the china and the aunt."

Wolviston nodded, then turned back to meet Clarissa's hot stare. St. Albans half expected the girl to go for the man's eyes with her claws. But they stood there, stalemated, each unwilling to give an inch.

Then something glimmered in the back of Wolviston's eyes. St. Albans disliked that glimmer. He preferred Wolviston to be a staid, predictable sort. He did not want to deal with a man like himself—a man who played by his own rules.

"If you won't let me pay," Wolviston said, turning to St. Albans, "what about a game? What say, since we've established that neither of us is a gentleman, that we dice? And we'll make her the prize?"

Interest leapt in St. Albans's jaded soul. But then Clarissa stepped forward, hands bunched into fists.

"You are not," she said, obviously struggling to hold onto her temper and poise, "going to dice or duel for me. I make my own choices."

Wolviston's smile turned into a sneer. "What sort of choice is it to throw your life away on him?"

St. Albans stiffened. "I beg your . . ."

"You stay out of this," Clarissa snapped, then whirled on Wolviston. "I am making a choice, sir, for passion. For more than the pretense you were willing to give me!"

"It was not all pretend," he said, his voice dropping low.

She gave a laugh. "No? What parts were not? Were you ever going to tell me which was which, my Lord Rake? Or did you think you could wait indefinitely? You think I am so easy to fool, after all?"

Wolviston met her stare, his own storming and dark. "There will never be a day when you do not matter to me."

Oh, damn the man, St. Albans thought. The time to get rid of the fellow had slipped right past. The fire danced again in Clarissa's blue eyes, but hesitancy lay there as well. He looked from Wolviston's bleak anguish to Clarissa's uncertainty, and a foolish whim rose in him.

It would be a novel sensation to act on such an impulse. Odd, but novel. And it would at least solve the problem of what to do with her, for it was better to have her gone now before she reverted back to that willing blandness.

He moved closer to her, dropping his voice seductively, acting before habit made him think better of it. "What do you want, Clarissa? Do you want him? Or do you still want a Grand Passion with me that will burn like a shooting star, blazing so sweet, and so hot for . . . well, for however long it does blaze?"

Starting to frown, she glanced from him to Wolviston. Then lifted her chin. "I still want a Grand Passion. I am not giving that up."

Wolviston stepped forward. "Have I asked you to give that up? Have I?"

Her lower lip quivered. She bit it and turned away. "You did not have to. I could feel the difference in how you kissed me when you asked me to be a wife."

St. Albans let out a laugh.

Evan shot the man a deadly look that sobered the fellow; then he came forward and took Clarissa's hand, tentatively at first, and then firmly in his grasp when she did not pull away.

"Clarissa, you may not have cause to believe me, but I think we are well beyond lies. I may not be able to offer you what St. Albans can. I certainly lack his experience in sin, and I do not know much about these Grand Passions. But I'd wager my soul there's something he has not said to you.

"He has not said that there is another kind of love beyond a fleeting passion. A deeper love. A love that rekindles itself. A love that does not burn like a star, but which is as endless as the sea, and which ebbs and rises and lasts beyond just this moment. I know about that love, for I fell in love with you the first I glimpsed you—yes, even with you scornful and proud, and so bewitching that it hurt. And I kept falling in love with you, again and again. When I saw you that first day in the park. Even when you were dancing on my heart, I was still fool enough to fall in love with you again."

"Fool enough," she said, her tone bitter. "So only fools fall in love with me?"

He dragged a hand through his hair, disordering it. "I don't know how to say the right things to you."

Looking at him, Clarissa hesitated. She still hated him—even more than ever. He had reached in and had taken apart that wall she had started to build against him. Just as she feared, she was weakening.

She gave a small sniff, and then pressed her lips tight. Oh, she wanted so wretchedly to hold onto her poise. She would feel too vulnerable without it. And yet . . . and yet . . .

She glanced at St. Albans, who stood there, cool and composed, looking faintly annoyed. Then she glanced at Wolviston. Regret darkened his gray eyes until they looked as storming as a winter's sky. His forehead bunched, and his mouth lay in a thin, strained line.

Then St. Albans said, his voice drawling, "You are a fool, Wolviston. She wants my desire more than she wants your love."

Anger kindled in her. "Neither of you understand. It's always about only one thing to you. It's love. Or it's desire. Or it's marriage. You put them into separate boxes, one for a wife and one for a mistress. Well, I want all those things together. I want a lover. And I want a husband. And I want a father for my children. And I want it all with someone who I can love so much that I forget to think about myself for thinking about him. I want kisses that leave my toes tingling, and shoulders to cry on, and warm arms around me when I am old."

Tears had sprung to her eyes. She started to brush them away, but then she had had enough. If they thought her an unsophisticated wretch, well, that's what she was at the moment. So she let the tears slide down her cheeks and glared at them, wishing they both would go to the devil.

Evan watched the play of emotions on Clarissa's face. Hope stirred in him, like water moving under spring ice. Beyond the haughty disdain that sparked in her eyes lay a certainty that he had never seen before. His heart tightened in his chest and he knew he'd done it again—he was falling in love with her. Here she was, standing in a rake's parlor, arguing about passion. She met life head-on, daring anything. And he loved her for it. How had he ever been idiot enough to think that being married to her would be a tame thing? He had known more adventure since meeting her than he had ever had in his entire life before.

"Clarissa . . ." he started to say, then broke off as she turned her sharp glare on him.

No, he was not doing that again. His words only got him into trouble.

"Devil take it," he muttered, and he swept her, squeaking and stiffening, into a crushing embrace.

He kissed her until he lost track of time and place. He kissed her until her struggling body softened against him. He kissed her until her arms wound around his neck and her lips parted and she breathed a sigh of surrender into his mouth.

When he pulled back, she stared at him, wide-eyed, the tears still glittering in her eyes and a smile trembling on her reddened lips.

Then she scowled like a fishwife. "Why did you not do that when you asked me to marry you?"

He grinned. "At the time I was trying to act as if I'd reformed into a gentleman. I should have known better. . . ." He let his words fade off as he lowered his mouth to hers again, eager to taste the spice of wine on her lips, and to soften her mood toward him. He tightened his hold on the curves that fit so well against his body.

St. Albans's loud throat-clearing intruded, and Evan looked up to glare at the man.

"Oh, stuff it, Wolviston," St. Albans said. "You look at me like that again and I shall blow your heart out. Now allow me to take my leave before you forget again that I am here."

Impatient to have the man gone, Evan loosened his grip on Clarissa and St. Albans took her hand. "My sweet mystery, I have recalled an urgent appointment in London—an immediate need for sin. Please make use of my house for as long as you wish. And I shall read the notice in the papers about your wedding with a regret for what we might have had." He gave her a smile. "It would have been memorable, my dear. Not forever, but memorable indeed."

Clarissa dimpled up at him. Then, unable to keep the happiness bottled inside, she flung her arms around his neck and kissed his cheek. "You are not really so awful, are you?"

St. Albans flicked her cheek with one finger. "Oh, I really am so awful. If you had not warmed within the quarter-hour, I had a dose of opiate ready to add to your brandy."

A chill slipped into her and she gave him a frown, but then Wolviston's arm curved over her shoulders, sheltering and warm, and St. Albans moved away.

The two men's stares measured each other—St. Albans's as if he were gauging just how much Wolviston had won from him that night, Clarissa thought, and Wolviston's arrogant and territorial. Pleasant tingles danced in her chest. Then she glanced up at Wolviston, at the strong line of his chin and the faint shadow of beard, and she could think only of how she wanted to trail her fingers across its contours.

St. Albans turned and walked to the door, then stopped and said to them, a wicked gleam in his eyes. "If he bores you, Clarissa, do let me know." With an elegant bow, he left.

Clarissa found herself at once trapped by possessive arms. "And if I ever find you anywhere near his door, I shall beat you."

"No, you shan't," she said, easing her arms free so she could smooth the lines from his forehead and tug his cravat straight—a difficult thing when his arms squeezed the breath from her, and his masculine scent left her light-headed. "Because if you ever, ever beat me I would run away from you."

His eyes darkened and his arms tightened around

her until he lifted her to her tiptoes. "Never run away from me. Never. Don't even say that in fun."

She tried to smile at him, but the desperation in his face left her unable to make light of it. "Then will you run away with me? Now? Please, Evan. Take me to Gretna tonight. Gallop off with me to the Scottish border to marry across the anvil. I want us to start as we mean to go on. Please, Evan. Do you love me so much that you cannot wait to marry me?"

He hesitated. She saw the doubt slip into his eyes, saw him start to weigh his duties.

"But, darling. What about your family? Your uncle and Lady Havers must be worried."

"No, they're not," she said, her happiness starting to dim. Oh, dear, he was not going to like this.

"They're not?" he asked, a puzzled frown creasing his forehead.

She bit her lower lip, then confessed. "I left a note. Only I knew they would worry if I mentioned Lord St. Albans, so I said I was running off with you, because I knew they rather approved of you."

His frown darkened. "You mean you laid the blame for your disappearance on me?"

"Well, I was not happy with you at the time. I wanted to hurt you. But I am very sorry, Evan. Really, I am. And if you really think we must, then we shall go back to London tonight and no one will know we have been gone, and we will be quite respectably married . . . if you like."

With a knot tight between his brows, Evan stared down at his love, his light, his devil. A dozen reasons why they ought to go back to London flitted through his mind. Her family. His own. Responsibilities. Duties. Society's opinions.

Then he took her face between his hands and looked deep into her eyes. What he saw was her need to know that he did love her—madly, badly, dangerously.

"I do love you," he said, then kissed her. And with a muffled curse he grabbed her hand. He started for the door, sweeping up his hat and greatcoat with his free hand.

"Evan, what is it? What's wrong?"

He stopped at the door and pulled her to him with a tug that caught her up against him so hard that she let out a small gasp of surprise. "Nothing's wrong. I'm a rake now, aren't I? And what better way to start a mad marriage than with a mad gallop for a sweet reward the following day?"

He swept her up and swung her about, kissing her, then said, "You may regret this night. It shall be a long, hard journey."

Grinning, she clung to him, her head spinning, her lips bruised, and her heart near to bursting. He did love her. He really did.

"I shall never regret anything with you!" she said, then lowered her chin to look up at him from under her lashes. "But must we wait until tomorrow for that sweet reward?"

He eyed her, one eyebrow lifted. "You are a wicked creature, Miss Clarissa Derhurst. And I can see that it is going to take years to reform you. At least it had better take years. Many, many, long years," he said, his mouth lowering to hers.

And when he released her lips, he swept her up in his arms and out into the darkness to claim that sweet reward.

AUTHOR'S NOTE

Since this is a novel, fact has been occasionally bent to suit fiction. There is no need, however, to dramatize the Byron scandal. However, the opinions of Lady Wolviston on the subject are her own—and it should be noted that Byron actually did some of his best work after he left England.

1816 proved to be a banner year for gossip in one other aspect. Not only did Byron's wife leave him—and then he England, with women trailing him to Dover for a last glimpse—but a month later, Mr. Brummell also quit the country. The cards had turned against him, and Dick Meyler exposed Brummell's inability to make good on a promise to pay £30,000 as his part of a joint money-making venture. Faced with arrest for debt, Brummell fled, leaving the unpopular Mr. Meyler to become known as "Dick the Dandy Killer."

Between these two major scandals, Evan and Clarissa's romp, and their hasty marriage, could easily be swept aside, allowing them to happily step back into Society whenever it suited them.

I love hearing from readers, and you can e-mail or write for a free bookmark with one of my favorite poems by Byron, *Stanzas for Music*, by writing:

Shannon Donnelly
PO Box 3313
Burbank, CA 91508-3313
read@shannondonnelly.com
http://www.shannondonnelly.com

Shannon Donnelly grew up with the perfect education for a Regency sportswoman, learning to ride, fence, and shoot (the last courtesy of an uncle who collected flintlocks). *A Dangerous Compromise* is her second Regency from Zebra. Her first, *A Compromising Situation,* won the Romance Writers of America's Golden Heart. Her abiding passions include—beside writing—a husband, three dogs, reading, gardening, and the ever-present horses in her life. She is currently at work on her next Regency, and will have a story out in the *Autumn Kittens Anthology,* October 2001.